VANILLA BREAKS

An erotic memoir

David Wade

Published by Xcite Books Ltd – 2016
ISBN 9781786154507

Copyright © David Wade 2016

The right of David Wade to be identified as the author of this work has been asserted by him in accordance with the Copyright, Designs and Patents Act 1988.

The names, occupations and locations of the real people appearing in this book have been changed; all the names are entirely fictional and do not refer to any living person of the same name.

All rights reserved. No part of this book may be copied, or transmitted in any form or by any means, electronic, electrostatic, magnetic tape, mechanical, photocopying, recording or otherwise, without the written permission of the publishers: Xcite Books, Ty Cynon House, Navigation Park, Abercynon, CF45 4SN

For Alice, without whom all hope would have been lost

There are more weak people than strong ones. The weak are legion. They don't see beyond the horizon. The world outside is where things come from, things that cause trouble, that jar the proper order of life. The weak aren't interested in thinking. Depths are frightening, long roads a journey without purpose where one could end up lost. Among the strong, only a few are worth paying attention to. Most are bullies. There are plenty of these bastards, pig-eyed and blustery little boys in big bodies. Or fish-eyed nasty bitches. They both revel in destroying lives. But there are others whose strength is of a much rarer kind. Not easy to find, because they reveal nothing. They are quiet. They often believe themselves to be much weaker than they are. To find one such as this is the most precious of discoveries.
  Steven Erikson

The fantasies, sexual urges, or behaviours must cause clinically significant distress or impairment in social, occupational, or other important areas of functioning in order for sexual sadism or masochism to be considered a disorder.
  Diagnostic and Statistical Manual of Mental Disorders, American Psychiatric Association

The most bitter remorse is for the sins we did not commit.
  Anon

Foreword

Prejudice has, since the dawn of time, been rooted in ignorance. I've fallen victim to it myself on a number of occasions. And I have certainly been guilty of casting it against others. Sometimes we just need to open our minds to what's out there, and the best way to do that is to stop blindly staggering behind tradition and misinformation, and to truly look and listen and try to understand the world around us.

After some pretty extensive research, I've discovered that numerous individuals are, even in these so-called "enlightened" times, still falling victim to sexual discrimination. And, commonly, in one particular aspect of it: kink. Many people have, over the years, been placed under investigation by their employers after having declared themselves (or having been "outed" by those they trusted to confide in) practitioners of BDSM. This doesn't include those who have been fired outright from their jobs. I am horrified and disappointed that this is the case, particularly in a society where people are supposedly free to do as they please in private; aside from breaking the law, of course. As with anything that is vastly misunderstood due to preconceptions and lies, people in the D/s scene seem often to be persecuted based purely on ignorance.

For the benefit of anyone who is unsure of any of

the above terminology – as I was when I began writing this – BDSM is a widely used abbreviation within the kink and fetish community. It is an amalgamation of three pairs of initials: BD stands for bondage and domination; DS (or D/s) represents domination and submission; and SM is sadism and masochism.

The names of places and characters in this book have been changed. I've done this not to protect myself (I don't rightly give ten flying fucks what the world thinks of me), but to protect those for whom I care. Revealing what I get up to in private, in all its glorious detail, could see my wife "Catherine" lose a career that she has worked incredibly hard to build and at which she excels. Perhaps if she were a housewife instead of an education professional, a bit of D/s activity would be considered a somewhat irreverent dalliance. But she works with children, so she's a target, simply by association with a writer whose story contains material potentially offensive to small-minded bigots.

I'm 43 years old. Not long ago I was a happily married man with a well-paying job, two bright and happy young children, and a nice house in a quiet village in suburban Buckinghamshire, England. And then, out of the blue, my world turned upside down. It has yet to be righted. In February of 2009 I was retrenched. Our savings – meagre to begin with – evaporated. Our mortgage was in danger of slipping with each passing month. Catherine started working even more ridiculous hours than she already had been in order to keep us afloat. But, bizarrely, following a lengthy discussion, it was decided that I would not actively seek a new job, but would instead become a househusband for a year or so to enable Catherine to further her chosen career. This decision resulted in me gradually sliding into a rut; stuck at home looking after two small children who seemed to my tired and fragile mind to be constantly bickering. I was wading through an existence that was slowly threatening to drive me insane. The dark thoughts and contempt for my fellow humans I had cultivated throughout my teenage years, but which had since – through mental discipline and sheer bloody mindedness – been reduced to a slightly annoying presence buried at the back of my consciousness, threatened to escape. And if that happened, nothing would turn out well.

Less than three years ago, I had virtually no idea what BDSM was. I have never in my life held any desire to inflict pain on another person in order to grant them sexual pleasure. Like most other people, I had a vague notion that this was essentially what the sordid and shadowy world of BDSM entailed. I was happy with my lot; happy to be an average man living an average life. And yet I became a Dominant, a damn good one by all accounts, with a suitcase full of tools and implements under my bed that I use to inflict pain and bestow pleasure on women who have willingly given me control over their bodies, minds, and emotions, at least for a short while. This journey from my old life to the new has, at times, threatened to break me; it is not something I ever would have expected, or wanted to go through if I'd been given the choice. Ironically, as my submissive sits here typing this for me, I find myself completely immersed in and utterly enraptured by the world of BDSM.

Having discovered this particularly wonderful nectar, I could never again go back to a life without kink, or try to behave as society would have me do, following ridiculous rules of etiquette in a restrictive, prejudiced "vanilla" world. I have seen the light. But instead of running from it as many others in a similar position may have done, I chose to embrace it. In doing so I have unearthed a person who I thought had long since ceased to be; I have rediscovered myself.

    This is my diary.

Introduction

Winter in England is one hell of a bad time to start experimenting with kink.

Catherine lay on the bed, flat on her stomach, her wrists bound with rope above her head. She wore a blindfold and nothing else. She was shaking, but I had no idea if that was due to the cold or her anticipation of what I was about to inflict upon her. She was breathing fast, so I figured it was the latter. I stood at the side of the bed, studying Catherine's face. Her expression appeared calm, which was a good thing given our situation.

I had been given the thick leather belt a few years previously – by Catherine, ironically (or perhaps intentionally, who knows?) – as a Christmas present. I'd never worn it. This gift was now wrapped around my right arm. I held the belt firmly in my right hand as my arm rested at my side. I felt nervous, anxious to make a start, yet petrified, because I was about to beat the hell out of the only woman I have ever loved. What were we doing? What had happened to the normal life we'd led only a few weeks ago? She wanted this, which made it OK ... didn't it? I lifted the belt slowly, quietly, until it was poised just behind my head. Was I really going to go through with this? How was this in any way going to be a pleasant experience for either of us?

Catherine had started to shake, a lot, and I realised with something close to panic that it wasn't actually very warm in the bedroom any more. Whatever I decided to do, it needed to be done quickly. I raised the belt slightly higher, inhaling in preparation for what was to come. Catherine stiffened – she must have been listening to my breathing in the silence of the room: the room where we had conceived both of our children; where we had held each other while discussing our lives, our dreams, our bright futures. I couldn't believe what was happening. It was all so surreal.

I brought the belt down with all my might, and the noise it made was deafening. Catherine's backside clenched as the blow struck. But instead of a cry of pain, she let out a moan of ecstasy. This reaction was as foreign to me as finding an elephant in my cornflakes. The feeling it stirred within me was indescribable. Exhilaration, perhaps, caused by an endorphin rush; a burst of adrenaline shooting through me in an instant. The emotional turbulence of that moment was overwhelming. It's strange, isn't it? Just when you start to think you know yourself, you discover you know nothing at all.

Part One
Dear Diary: Brazil – 1984 to 1998

14 July 1984

Today Marco suggested I should start writing a diary. Marco and I have known each other for over a decade, been in the same classes for more than half that time. He's my *bro*, my best mate, my main man. So here I am, writing a diary. Marco told me that doing this would help me sort out my head. Apparently it worked for his sister who's had all sorts of issues, the fat cow. Stopping eating would have helped her sort that shit out a lot sooner. And possibly a lot more successfully, too.

So. A diary. Here we are then. So far I've done five pages of superhero drawings and now I'm writing this bullshit. Sixteen years old, and writing in a little black book like some emotionally unstable little girl who needs to tell the world how much she loves Billy but Billy doesn't know she exists and now she wants to kill herself. Boo hoo.

Fuck it. I don't have time for this.

3 February 1996

God, did I really write that? Wow. OK. Twelve years ago I wrote that. I even vaguely remember Marco's sister. She wasn't actually fat at all, but I just didn't like her. Or maybe I liked her more than I led myself to believe. I was such a hormonal little bastard at school.

Weird that I didn't throw away this diary. Just found it way down at the bottom of a box that Mom sent to me because she's finally moving out of that shitty old house. I love the superhero drawings –

they're bloody hilarious. I remember I wanted to be an artist, back then. But instead, having sold my soul for money, I'm happily employed as a mediocre web developer at a mediocre IT company. I guess that's why I'm writing in here again – it helps me to get away from the monotony of my life for a while. Tracey (my current girlfriend) is away for a week and I'm bored. So do I go out for a burger with Juan and Emilio, or do I look through my old shit? Well, here I am. I'm such a loser.

So, what else has happened in 12 years? Well, for one I've moved on from being an emo kid. OK, maybe not entirely. But life is much nicer now that I have a steady job and a hot girlfriend. I was in the army for a while – two years that I'll never get back and fuck you kindly to the Brazilian government for conscripting me to that. As if I wasn't already mentally unstable enough, they decided I needed a bit of brainwashing and indoctrination on how to kill people with guns. Thanks. No really, thanks. But fuck you very much. Prime years of my life gone; plenty of time and effort wasted for no good reason at all. Anyway, it's over. No need to spend more time thinking about that utterly shitty period of my life.

7 February 1996

Hm. I was just getting stuck into a good bit of ranting there, but then Juan phoned and invited me over and that was the end of my diary entry and my nostalgic bitching session. Hell, I actually enjoy writing. Who knew? Maybe Marco wasn't full of shit all those years ago, after all. I wonder what happened to him.

We lost touch after school. I should look him up, some time. Or maybe not. Some things are best left alone.

So yeah; army, college, girlfriend, job. I guess this is where my life as a "responsible adult" starts. I do so love being shoved into this little box that society has created for me. "Society". Hah! As if there's anything socially acceptable about any of us. The human race has outlived its usefulness. And what purpose did we serve in the first place? We're the only species that kills or exploits those weaker than us for financial gain. We're "self-aware", or so we proclaim in our immense arrogance. And that's our excuse to do what we like to a planet that has struggled through billions of years of evolution until it reached a point where it could support life, only for that life to then turn on it and systematically erode the poor spinning bastard into uselessness.

I've lost track again. But then what's the point of a diary, if not to reveal our innermost thoughts and feelings? It's a damn sight cheaper than a therapist.

13 March 1996

OK, here's something worth writing about: a first for me. A few days ago – it was last Saturday – Trace and I were eating lunch on the patio. We'd finished a bottle of white wine between us. It was hot, one of those days when the humidity makes you stick to yourself. We had fans going. Tracey was wearing a thin ankle-length sun dress. All of a sudden she stretched one leg out and rested it on me, and then bent her other leg, so that her foot was on her chair.

Which was nice, in itself. But then the fan blew her dress up a bit, and as it did so, Tracey yanked the rest of it all the way up to reveal that she wasn't wearing anything underneath. Thank God we're walled off from any neighbours, or they would have had something other than our loud music to complain about. I was shocked, but seriously aroused. Trace has never been promiscuous, or especially interested in sex – at least, not after the initial few months together. I must have uttered some kind of surprised comment, because Tracey asked me if what she was doing bothered me. I replied no, of course not. So then, *then*, she leaned across and whispered that she wanted me to fuck her in the arse! I mean … What? Where did that come from? Here's my lovely, sweet, gentle girl, suggesting that we do something I've only ever seen in porn magazines. Maybe it was the wine, or the heat, or both, but I had never seen her this horny before. But I was definitely interested. I grinned like an idiot, and then told her to turn around and lean over her chair. She looked surprised and told me that she hadn't meant, like, right here and now. She was concerned that the neighbours would see us. That couldn't happen, unless they were on a ladder looking over the eight-foot-high concrete walls. Tracey still looked sceptical, but I grabbed her waist and spun her around. I could tell that she was still hesitant, but she stood there, bent over, with her hands on the chair's armrest and her dress hitched up over her back. I was incredibly hard at that moment. I'd never had anal sex before (not given or received it, for the record), but the whole idea of doing this – specifically the thought that it's a bit dirty and illicit –

was such a turn-on. I fumbled around for a bit, trying to penetrate her, but she was tight. I thought about going inside the house to get some lube, but then I noticed that she was absolutely dripping between her legs. I shoved my thumb into her pussy, and then into her backside. She gasped. For good measure I started fucking her vagina to lubricate myself. And then I removed my thumb and thrust my cock firmly into her arse. She squealed, in what I hoped was a good way. The rush of adrenaline, the excitement; the thrill of forbidden fruits … It was all unbelievably sexy. I came within seconds, and stood there, listening to myself huff and snort like some wild animal. Tracey asked me if I had come, and I told her yes, and it had been amazing. She pushed away from me and went inside, and didn't speak to me again for the rest of that day. I'm guessing it was because she'd expected me to last a bit longer, but there was no way I could control that. Or, maybe, she had wanted some foreplay. But the situation had snowballed, and all I could think about at the time was being inside her. I don't really know what I'd done wrong, and I will probably never have any idea. Women are a strange breed. If I could get inside their heads, to have even an inkling of how they think, I'd be a very happy man.

26 May 1996

Tracey's left me. Well, technically I left her – she can have the apartment and every fucking thing in it. None of that shit means anything to me anymore. Maybe I'll go back and collect a few CDs and clothes at some stage. Or maybe I won't even bother with that, and I can avoid seeing her cheating, slutty face ever again. God, she's a cunt. If anybody ever deserved being called that, she does. How many times did she reassure me that she hated hugely muscled men? Or perhaps that was just a dig at my skinny-arsed self, and I was too dumb to catch the hints. She also told me she'd stopped smoking about three years ago.

Last week I got off work early and went to visit her, at the restaurant where she works as a waitress, and I found her standing outside, smoking. Not only that, but she had her arm around some fuck who must spend his entire useless existence working out at a gym. He doesn't even have a neck, the greasy twat. They were having such a good time they didn't see me, so I turned around and left again. Good to know my life has been built on lies and deception. Brilliant, in fact. She can just fuck off. Seriously. Why do people have to be so absolutely fucking rubbish? I feel like crying, partly because what I thought was an amazing relationship is gone, but also because I feel so utterly betrayed. I'm an idiot for believing anything she ever told me. There must have been signs. I always thought I was good at picking up hints, at spotting a lie. Seems I wasn't. I guess I just suck at everything.

3 December 1996

Just reread that last entry. Very eloquent, indeed. I was once told that if you need to use an expletive more than once in any comment, you seriously need to re-evaluate your grasp of the language. I wasn't really trying to be eloquent, though. I was just miserable and angry. I guess I could edit out the nasty bits, but that would be defeating the purpose of recording a diary. I haven't seen Tracey again, and good riddance to her. She can have all the CDs – they were mostly soft rock crap anyway, reserved for simpering guests (mostly her new-age weirdo friends) at dinner parties. It's been a few months now, and I'm still upset and disappointed by what she did. I guess I'll never get over it. Betrayal is pretty tough to forgive.

31 December 1996

Admittedly, I am an angry and embittered man. I've always been a loner. As a youth I was often antisocial and reclusive. In my teenage years I found solace within a select group of people who seemed to understand how my head worked: Goths. But most of them didn't have a clue what I felt. A slight streak of rebellion and angst does not a Goth make. My army psychiatrist told me I was a manic depressive with psychopathic tendencies, just because I attacked a fellow recruit. The fuck was attempting to grab my cock at the time, and had one hand around my throat. But the shrink didn't want to hear about that part of it. So I got labelled with some pretentious psycho-babble bullshit. Yet again the world is witness to persecution with no valid cause and a rampant lack of facts. God, how I hate some people.

It's incredibly difficult maintaining anything other than a simpering grimace as I attempt to wade through this banal, plodding craptitude that we call life. We're taught from the start to smile through adversity, to turn the other cheek while others who are stronger, richer, more arrogant and less caring plough right over us. And why? It makes us better people, apparently. I'd laugh, but for the fact that I have spent my life watching moronic, selfish, bloated, socially inappropriate cretins rise above me in all walks of life. Am I stronger? Am I a better person for it? Perhaps "bitter" would be more appropriate.

I'm a wretched git. This is a fact. I'm not some teenager with a hormonal imbalance who needs to find an outlet for their frustrations. I don't dye my hair black and blue and purple and have rings in every dangling appendage on my body. Yet I suppose I do share some of the more inward traits of what defines a rebel. I remember when I first discovered my "alternative" tendencies. Politics meant nothing to me when I was growing up. There will forever be some inept wanker running a country into the ground. I do believe that most of these people probably start off thinking they can make a difference; possibly do some good for the citizens who voted for them due to well-meaning promises of a better life. But we're all sheep. We follow the alphas who make the greatest noise. Well, I say "we", but that again is a generalisation. As I said, I'm not interested in politics. Or religion. I follow nobody – not now, not ever. I'll say no more about either of those two subjects, since they tend to drive some people into a frenzy and give them an excuse to start wars or butcher thousands and have, since time immemorial, led to nothing other than misery for billions of innocents. My beliefs are skewed from the norm, I wear black clothing because I like it, and I question rules when I think they may be unfair or moronic. And therefore I am labelled a troublemaker. Why? Because I dare to think for myself. Does that make me "alternative"? Does that make me a rebel? Or, God forbid, an anarchist? Am I uncaring? Do I attack my neighbours and cause shit? Not at all. Do I not wish to engage in the world around me? Of course I do – to say otherwise would be to deny that I am human. But with regard to getting involved in politics and religion, any attempt to challenge the system is pointless. The world is run by political, religious and business leaders, and so long as these people are enjoying their lives of comfort, looking down at the rest of us from their lofty ivory towers, there is no point at all in fighting the powers that be.

Christ, look at me wittering on. So much for a diary. Looks like I'm writing a fucking book.

4 November 1997

I've read a few interesting articles over the past few years regarding rape. Disturbing articles. Aside from the fact that the act of rape in itself is disturbing, that is. What I've read has mostly been stories from the international press, regarding some male attitudes towards this violent practice. Very often, the views of the male witnesses – and sometimes the perpetrators – interviewed have been based on geographical or religious grounds. In other words, blinkered viewpoints steeped in tradition; a patriarchal belief that men somehow take precedence over women.

These men have been raised on the beliefs of their forefathers. Browbeaten over the course of generations by mindless indoctrination, they are led to believe that they are superior in some way, and it is therefore their right to control the "weaker" sex.

These same people seem to think that rape is somehow justified, for whatever reasons may suit them at the time. I've read comments along the lines of, 'She looked at another man outside our marriage.' (A marriage that she may or may not have actually wanted or chosen for herself in the first place). So that's an excuse for the entire male population of her village to rape and beat her? Or perhaps she wore provocative clothing. Or maybe the girl ignored (or, God forbid, laughed at) the fool's bumbling attempts to chat her up. Whatever the case, certain men will always use some feeble excuse for why they couldn't control their wanton sexual urges. They will find a way to blame the victim. What these simple-minded buffoons fail to grasp is that entire lives are shattered forever by their brief gratification, and their pathetic lust and desire to dominate another human being. I am often ashamed and disgusted that I am a male of this species. Why did we ever bother coming down from the trees?

12 January 1998

The lack of writing recently is because I've met someone. Her name is Catherine. She's just completed a college degree in teaching special needs children or something. I should probably pay more attention to the specifics, but I've been far too busy getting to grips with her other, more interesting aspects. We've been doing the typical dating thing: lots of nights at the cinema watching rubbish films; lots of meals out; lots of sitting in parks drinking wine and watching the sun set. And lots of evenings at her apartment, doing unspeakable things on a thick, shaggy rug in front of her fireplace. It's so clichéd, yet it's exciting as hell. This feels good. It feels right. We have a connection, something I haven't felt with anyone since Tracey. I'm not thinking too much about that, though; just enjoying what it is and what we have right now. Let's see where this goes.

21 February 1998

Again with the lack of diary entries. I've just been too busy. Things have taken off spectacularly with Catherine. We get along incredibly well. I can't really say much more, aside from the fact that she has every quality I've always wanted in a partner: she's funny, sexy, intelligent, and beautiful. We've even done the whole meet-and-greet thing with our respective families and friends. Life is so good right now.

21 July 1998

Hey diary. What news? Not much. Everything is just sort of plodding along. Cat and I have fallen into a bit of a routine, which is cool. We're renting a nice place in a quiet suburb; we're both working, seeing a few friends here and there, but mostly just chilling out and enjoying life together.

All quiet on the writing front. Guess I haven't had much to say. Hell, I haven't had much to think about, either. But I had to write what's in my head today, and I thought this would be a good place to do it. Based on some of my previous entries, this diary's legacy as a dumping ground for my inane and meandering thoughts remains sound.

When I was younger I was inspired. I thought I could do anything. Given the opportunity I could have conquered the world. But I was never given the opportunity. Probably precisely because I was young. Politicians all seemed so very old and the law seemed to always favour the rich and the powerful. Fairness and justice seemed reasonable concepts, yet failed somehow in practice. And as I sit here now, having experienced so many more years of life since those early days of wonder and innocence, I find myself pondering whether I can revitalise any of the ideals I aspired to back then. Sadly, I think I am now less capable of achieving any of those things. Back then, when I probably *could* have achieved them, I was way too busy doing exactly what young people are supposed to do; being dumb and having fun. I drank too much; I smoked the occasional joint, got involved in the occasional fight, and ate junk. And I didn't care about anything other than sex. Or rather, how little I was getting, especially as I watched everyone around me seemingly enjoying it in abundance. Sleep was deep and restful, music was amazingly loud, and the sun had never shone so brightly. I was embracing the world, yet at the same time keeping it at a safe distance. I was fearless, untouchable. The future was far away, so far that it didn't bear thinking about. My memories of that time – of the specifics – are lacking, probably due to too much alcohol. Yet a lingering feeling of ultimate freedom remains. I guess that's called nostalgia. I shouldn't be so melancholy; I have a great life with a beautiful woman, a good job, and a fine bunch of friends and family. But even so, I can't help but wonder if I'll ever feel as alive again as I did back in my youth.

18 August 1998

Ironic how I wrote in my previous entry about what a good job I have. I've just been thinking about my boss, and how much I'd like to fuck him up. He's an over-privileged wanker who dresses in fancy clothes and drives a brand-new, luxury sports car paid for by his millionaire daddy. What a prick. Maybe he thinks that driving an expensive car makes him more attractive to others, or elevates him above the rest of society. Although I'm sure it actually does achieve that in some cases. There probably are people out there who are impressed by that sort of display; the kind of people who find kissing someone's arsehole a rewarding pastime. But all I want to do to the pompous twat is corner him in a dark alleyway and beat him to within an inch of his life.

I guess for anyone reading this (perhaps my unsuspecting grandchildren, when they delve into their parents' attic someday and find this tattered old diary written by their mentally unstable granddad who died an early death from a stress-related coronary), I should explain my rage. I'd like to think I'm just jealous that my boss has a lot of money. That explanation would be easy. But it's more than that. It's the way he acts, how he treats people. How he exudes arrogance, believing himself to be above anyone else. Doesn't he understand how insignificant a speck he is in the order of the universe?

Too many people are obsessed with money, with appearances. What they fail to realise is that the image they're projecting is massively negative. Perhaps their peers slap them on the back down at the golf club as they sip their gin and tonics and relate stories of how many peons they trod on during the day. After which they all indulge in a session of snapping jockstraps and wrestling naked on the granite shower tiles. Hatred is never pretty, but it does tend to conjure up some amusing scenarios.

3 September 1998

I really do need to cut down on the vitriol. All this internal anger is not doing me any good. I can't change society, or the way people live their lives. It has always been the way of the world that some people will kill for a slightly larger slice of the pie. It's all about self, and fuck the rest. I was raised to respect others, to treat everyone equally, to be patient and kind, and to live and let live. Many others were never taught those basics, and are poorer for it. Unfortunately, some people they interact with will suffer due to that. These ignorant fucks will go to their graves having lived amazing lives, full of privileges and wonders that we less fortunate millions can only ever dream of. The world is not fair. Nobody ever promised that. And it never will be. I guess I just need to learn to live with that.

6 September 1998

Catherine and I were a bit shaken today. Did I mention that Cat is working as an intern? I meant to make a note of that earlier, but I was probably too busy ranting about something inconsequential. Anyway, she was walking back to her car from the faculty building early this evening when she saw another woman being attacked right in front of her. Some shithead wearing a balaclava had his hand over the woman's mouth and was trying to drag her into a wooded corner on one side of the lot. Cat saw it happening and screamed, and then ran at the guy. What the fuck was she thinking? Thank God he turned and ran, or who knows what could have happened? Or what would have happened to the victim if Cat hadn't spotted them. The police arrived eventually and took statements, but of course nothing will come of it. Nothing ever does. Scary shit, man. Needless to say, Cat is a bundle of nerves. She doesn't want to go back to the school again and I can't say I blame her. This country's turning to shit.

30 September 1998

Catherine and I are looking into moving overseas. Things over here are bloody rubbish and only seem to be getting worse: crime, corruption, pollution, and so on and so on. Bullshit. We pay taxes, and for what? Just last year a friend of mine was shot on the way to fetch his kid from school. Thank God his injury was superficial. The cops were disinterested in his account of what happened, and he hasn't heard a thing from them since. I've had enough. Both my parents and grandparents are British, so we can get into the United Kingdom quite easily. We'll need to get married, so that Cat will also be eligible for an ancestry visa, but that's easily done. Neither of us has ever wanted a lavish wedding, much to our families' dismay, so the whole event will just be an exercise in paperwork. Everyone close to us is miserable at the prospect of us leaving, but we need to think of our future. Especially if we plan to have children someday. So, yeah. Interesting times ahead, I reckon.

Part Two
Dear Diary: United Kingdom – 1999 to 2009

22 February 1999

We've moved to the United Kingdom, for all the reasons I stated previously. Brazil was becoming just a little bit too unbearable. Crime is spiralling over there; the government is intent on lining its own pockets with the millions allocated to helping the poor, and massive corporations continue to profit from the hard labour of the masses. I was surrounded by poverty on the one hand, and excessive wealth and arrogance on the other. Catherine and I decided that we wanted to begin a new life away from the negative bullshit that seemed so prevalent in our everyday existence. The environment is toxic there, and we refuse to raise children in that sort of society. We've sold the few things we owned, obtained our residency visas, and moved. So here we are. Welcome to Britain!

26 February 1999

I'm sitting here (sorry, I should change that to *I'm sat here*, which seems to be the correct way of saying it in this country), and I'm watching some fat fuck inhale a meal consisting of sausages, eggs, bacon, chips, white bread, and baked beans. Jesus! Does he even have a clue what he's doing to himself? Can nobody afford mirrors anymore? That guy has more chins than any one human being could possibly put to good use.

I'm at a café inside a supermarket, drinking some shit that they probably imagine passes for coffee, and jotting down my sad thoughts on a paper notepad. I'm also contemplating whether or not to eat this awfully forlorn-looking baguette that's slowly disintegrating on a plate in front of me. The baguette was the only reasonable option on the shelf; the only item that hadn't yet grown new life of its own. Now that I'm faced with this thing on a plate before me, I'm not entirely sure I'm actually capable of eating it. So, strike one: the food here sucks.

A month or so before we left Brazil, Catherine managed to get a telephonic interview for an entry-level teaching job in the UK, at a college here in Northern Ireland. She aced her interview. The people she spoke to seemed very eager to have her here, and so they arranged a post for her, as well as staff accommodation for us both within the campus grounds. The reason they were so eager, we now realise, is that the college itself is so dire, and the area so very deprived, that they would probably accept anyone at all, regardless of their qualification or education.

I haven't been so lucky on the work front, but it's early days yet. Even though we don't have much money, I need to buy myself a computer as soon as possible and start sending out my CV. No idea what the market is like for web developers in Ireland, but I guess I'll find out soon enough. I also need to start writing. Which is a great concept, but for the lack of story ideas. At the very least, I need to get my diary online. Paper is so very yesterday.

4 May 2002

Yet again, time flies and years pass in the blink of an eye. My last entry mentions buying a computer. Which I did, not too long after I wrote that. We got an internet connection, and I immediately started applying for jobs. But, because the area is so deprived, work was incredibly scarce. Also, Catherine only had a year-long contract and we didn't know where we'd be situated geographically after that, so I couldn't commit to permanent employment. I became bored, and made the mistake of starting to play computer games. Goodbye, ambition; goodbye, urge to do anything useful or constructive.

Eventually Catherine had to start applying for new jobs, and we decided we'd like to live in England so that we'd be close to friends of ours who had also relocated from Brazil a few years ago. I decided that I would begin looking for work near to where they were located, in a place called Aylesbury in the south of England. If I did find a job, Cat could then start narrowing her search to wherever my place of employment was. As it turns out, once I started searching again in earnest, I quickly found work. Catherine started applying for jobs soon after that, and a month later we had relocated to a quiet little village not too far from Aylesbury town centre.

My job is great, but work is often sparse. So I have a lot of free time at my desk. While we were still in Ireland I started transferring my diary into electronic format. I now carry a flash drive on my key ring and will probably make occasional entries during my "downtime" at work. I guess I'll trash the physical copy of my diary at some point. Just thinking about doing that makes me sad, somehow. But electronic format means I can store my thoughts pretty much anywhere, and at any time. I'm wondering if this will prompt me to write more often. Probably not, is my guess. I never have anything useful to say anyway. I'll attempt to write when I have something to write about, or when I think of it.

20 November 2002

Hello, diary. Checking out old folders on my computer because I'm upgrading, and I just found you again. So much has changed since those first entries I wrote. I've just been rereading some of it, and remembering my life as a teenager. I recall often thinking that the human race would never make it this far. We have such a propensity for killing each other off in the thousands – it's the one thing we're really good at, as a species. Yet instead of having wiped ourselves off the face of the planet with nuclear weapons, we have the internet. Who ever saw *that* coming? Life continues to surprise me, which is pretty special. I had started to consider myself beyond surprises. It's sweet, in a way, still being so naïve and wide-eyed at my age.

31 March 2004

We had a kid! Wow. Fucking incredible. Life is insane right now. I've never felt so tired. So, yeah, there you go. I said I'd write when I had something to write about. Here it is then. I need sleep. Oh, it was a boy. We called him Robert. He's perfect. And so is Cat. Yet another step up this mad ladder we call life.

01 January 2006

Jesus, I can't believe how time flies. Robert is already almost two years old. I haven't even thought about writing again until now. Life has just been insanely difficult and busy. Having a child completely changes everything. I wish somebody had warned me about that. Every part of me is screaming for a return to my quiet, selfish life, spending all my time and money on my own wants and needs. But that's impossible; you can never go back. People say kids are great, that you'll forget how life used to be before you had them. Uh … Really? I'm still waiting for that to happen. As gorgeous as my little boy is, I miss my old life.

12 August 2007

Kid number two has arrived. Another boy, but this one's of the screaming, angry variety. We think there must be something wrong with him because he hasn't stopped crying since he popped out. He occasionally sleeps, but only long enough to lull us into thinking we can finally get some sleep ourselves. So yet again I find myself questioning our incredible stupidity for deciding to have children. Why do people do this? To continue our "line", and to carry on the family name? What for? Our first child destroyed my sanity and serenity, and now he's getting to an age when he's becoming a little person, instead of a shitting bundle of noise, and we can start to enjoy him, we decide to have another one? To go through that trauma all over again? Lack of sleep, constant noise and chaos ... God! Is there anything in life more stressful than a newborn baby who never shuts the fuck up? I doubt it. I'm so ridiculously tired right now.

27 May 2008

How can two children from the same parents be so very, very different? It has to be said, with all sincerity, that if we'd had James first, I would have had my nuts removed. I had always thought that Robert was loud and troublesome ... Jesus. If I'd had any inkling how foul and unpleasant a small person could be, I would have thought twice (and then some) about having a second child. James' arse is the back door to hell, and that's one of his finer attributes. What a hideous little creature he is. I can't recall ever being that naughty. But then again, remembering yesterday is a stretch for me, much less trying to recall my behaviour as a toddler. Diaries are good for that; having a read over stuff that happened in the past, and remembering those times fondly. Or sometimes, not so much.

12 October 2008

There should be a practical book on parenthood. Never mind all the crap you read in a thousand assorted books about how to whisper to the mother's tummy, or drink yak's milk in preparation, or various other bits of crap that's generally fobbed off as "information" – fuck that. What people need to know are the hard facts: sleepless nights, the loss of all freedom and individuality, a constant lack of funds, endless noise, misery, mess, and occasional lapses into insanity. Thinking about becoming a parent? Go to a shopping mall. Right now. Before you enter, buy an ice cream. Hold it out in front of you, and then drop it down your shirt and onto your shoes. Then go into a supermarket. Remove a few random items from the shelves and either place them in other people's trolleys or put them back onto the shelves, but in different places to where they came from. Or else simply drop them onto the floor and stamp on them a little. Be sure to throw a few glass bottles onto the floor, taking care to splash yourself with the reddest and stickiest juice in the process. Do this over and over, at least twice a week, and you'll be ready – at least in part – to procreate.

04 July 2008

My God, why can't kids listen? I swear I may as well speak to my arse. It's more likely to answer, too, and whatever comes out will probably make more sense than my kids. It is my greatest desire that my children someday create offspring of their own who are as unruly as they are (if not worse), and who plague their lives with chaos. Is that uncharitable? Like I give even the tiniest fuck right now.

13 February 2009

I've been made redundant. Two weeks ago I was called in to my manager's office. I knew what was coming. I think I may have mentioned somewhere earlier that work was sparse. Which is not my fault; I'm not a salesperson. I can't create tasks for myself, and I won't pretend to be busy or lie on my timesheets. Anyway, the writing's been on the wall for a while now, so it was no surprise at all when I was told my particular post was no longer required within the company. I got a decent redundancy package, which we used to pay off Cat's new car.

Cat and I have talked about options for the future. She's just starting a two-year Master's degree in some high-echelon academic field, which will apparently help enhance her CV when she eventually starts applying for a senior teaching post. Due to this, and because James in still in preschool, we've decided that I won't start searching for a new job just yet, but will instead stay home and look after the house and the kids. It's an attractive option, having some time out of an office environment, and spending time with the kids. My mum's concerned, because "a man's place is not in the home, or looking after children". I just laughed at her. Traditionalist ideas are so quaint, but not really relevant in today's society. Anyway, Cat and I have made a deal; she's on her way to great things, and I'm her support unit. I feel a bit shitty that I'm not out there earning, but let's see how this goes. I could always start applying for jobs again in future, if money is getting tight.

16 March 2009: Retrospective

This entry has been inserted after the actual date it occurred. The reason for this is that the event I'm about to describe seemed so trivial, so irrelevant, that I didn't even think about it again, after it had happened. Yet it turned out to be the starting point of what was about to become the absolute, without a doubt, worst time of my life. It was on this day that my world would change forever, turning my life around and changing the person I was to the man I am today. And I didn't even know it.

I was lying in bed, reading. Catherine was running a bath. She came into the bedroom and started to get undressed. Then she stopped, reached into the top drawer of her bedside table, and handed me a few pieces of paper. She told me to have a look through the pages and, when she had returned from her bath, to let her know what my thoughts were. She said all of this very matter-of-factly, not looking in the least like any of this was very important. I looked at what she'd given me: *A History of Spanking*. Five pages, apparently torn from a magazine, detailing various techniques of how to smack a woman's backside. The writing was accompanied by illustrations, from a bawdy Victorian sketch of a lady with her skirts raised, being whipped with a cane, to a modern-looking photo of a woman being hit with a wooden paddle. I read about three pages of the article, and then lost interest and put it into my own bedside drawer.

When Cat came into the bedroom after her bath, she asked me what I'd thought. I told her it was intriguing, and asked why she'd given it to me. She asked me if I'd be interesting in trying something like that sometime. I replied that we could do, but that it wasn't something I'd ever really been interested in. I'd heard about sadomasochism, of course, but only infrequently, in crime novels and tabloids. It's mostly referred to as a bit of kinky fun to spice your sex life up a bit. Of course, I've also seen my fair share of porn, over the years, some of which featured women in handcuffs or having their arses caned. None of those stories or images had ever stirred any erotic feelings within me, and I wasn't at all interested in learning more about the practice. It was something that other people did, and I was happy to leave them to it.

After this exchange I started reading my novel again, so I'm not entirely sure what Cat's reaction was to my indifference. As far as I was aware, she just said, 'OK,' and that was that. Perhaps if she'd discussed it with me a bit further, or had given me even the tiniest bit of context, things could have turned out very, very differently.

8 March 2009

So far, so good. I've found I actually enjoy spending time with the kids, aside from the occasional tantrum from James, or Robert's sulky moodiness. They're both out of the house for a few hours each day – Rob at school and James at the preschool down the road – so I have some time for housework, and an hour or so to myself to watch crap on telly or play computer games. I really should be trying to write. I have an idea for a novel, but it really needs a lot more thought and planning. Hopefully I'll get around to that some time. I don't really have anything else useful to do.

Catherine is having to do private tuition at a posh college in London, to make up for my lack of earnings. She says she enjoys the drive and she's gaining valuable experience that will look good on her CV. At least the pay is good. I hate that she's in this position, but it's a choice we've made, and so far we both seem fine about it. I hope that lasts.

22 April 2009

The trouble with not suffering fools is that you're tested to the ends of your limits on a daily basis. Life is a lesson in patience. It is a lesson in which I don't appear to be learning very well. The mums at the school ... Oh! My! God! Despicable harridans. Why, for the love of the baby Jesus, do they have to stand in the very centre of the only fucking pathway into the school while they discuss their inconsequential shit? Every sodding day I trip over the shrubbery at the side of the gates as I try to squeeze past these fucking idiots, carefully trying to avoid touching them lest I'm hauled before a magistrate on harassment charges. They are just the sort of people who would do that. Today I finally lost my rag and bumped into one of them (harder than I'd intended, I hasten to add) and got a very audible 'How rude!' from the slag. Yes, I'm the rude one, impeding the progress of every other parent taking their kid to school, with my fat arse planted in the most inconvenient spot possible. I ignored her. Maybe, tomorrow, she'll stand somewhere else. Maybe, but most likely not. Mind you, aside from being a stupid, arrogant bitch, she's pretty hot. So maybe, tomorrow, I'll just have to bump into her again. By accident, of course.

**Part Three
Dear D/s Diary**

3 March 2010

We're going on vacation, in the midst of Catherine's master's degree; precious time that would probably be better spent at a library. But I guess she needs the break. And her parents are coming all the way from Brazil to accompany us, which I wouldn't miss for the world. Sarcasm, much?

Catherine's master's degree has cost in the region of three thousand pounds – money that we absolutely do not have. And, on top of that, it has meant that she has spent every conceivable spare hour in libraries or coffee shops, trying to research and write the dissertation part of the damn thing. This, in turn, means that she hasn't had time to do much private tuition, and the finances are starting to take a serious dive. All of which has served to strain our relationship slightly. The boys miss their mum. I miss having any time at all to myself. And Catherine misses having any time at all for anything other than work. What a fucking mess. So actually, but for the money issue, maybe a holiday isn't such a bad idea after all. Time will tell.

13 March 2010

We've hit the Mediterranean. A summary of our holiday so far: manic kids, ice creams smeared on the walls of our crappy villa, visiting boring places, and dealing with rude locals. I won't say where we are for fear of being sued by their tourist board (do they even have such a thing? God knows, they need all the marketing help they can get!), except that it's a small island where almost nobody speaks English. Why here? It was cheap. Cheap and crap seem invariably to go together.

15 March 2010: The Revealing

My whole world is fucked. Upside-down, turned around, fucked up, fucked.

Catherine's parents gave us a night to ourselves, offering to stay in and babysit the kids. Once the boys were tucked into bed we headed out, walking through the little seaside village looking for a restaurant. We found one, and it should have been an amazing evening – good weather, wonderful food, a lovely bottle of chilled white wine. But then, after dessert, Catherine drops a fucking load on me. She tells me that she's got this SM thing going on, says she's been signing up to internet forums and reading and chatting and is now in contact with some guy she met on God only knows what kind of dodgy website. Er … what? I'm shaking as I write this. This person's name is Simon. Like I care. Cat and Simon have been discussing her "submissive side", and he has been very good at explaining everything that she has wanted to know about herself for so many years. What the fuck? Oh, apparently she tried to tell me she was into kinky shit, a while ago. She gave me some pages to read, all about the history of spanking. I vaguely remembered her doing so, but without any explanation of what it was all about, or the obvious, fucking massive issues involved. So it's my fault, then. I'm to blame for having my wife consciously go to some stranger, and ask him to verbally fuck her, on chat forums and over the phone. I can't even describe how I'm feeling right now. Jesus.

16 March 2010

OK, so obviously, this has been bothering Catherine for quite some time now. Since she was a child, apparently. How lucky am I to be the recipient of her coming out? Why couldn't this have happened with one of her previous boyfriends, before she and I had established a life together?

After Cat had told me what was going on, last night, I didn't have much to say at all. I wasn't actually angry while she was telling me all of this, just confused. I had a lot to think about. I got home, and sat down at the dining room table, and wrote that previous entry. My head was – obviously – filled with too many thoughts, all of which were spinning around madly, with nowhere to go. So I regurgitated what I was thinking and feeling, none of which made sense at the time, onto a piece of paper.

But, after I'd written that, I completely surprised myself by actually feeling calm about it. I went to the bedroom. Cat was still awake. She told me that she loved me, more than anything, and that she wanted to grow old with me. She explained that this was something she'd always had inside her, and that, for the first time she was starting to understand what it was all about. She wanted me to know that it was a completely separate part of her and that, when she was with me, she was with me – completely. Simon was helping her understand, and deal with, the Dominant/submissive or "D/s" side of her persona, but that was all. It wasn't a relationship, and she had no feelings for him whatsoever. He had – at her insistence – started to make her do things that had excited her. I felt enraged, but also incredibly stupid. I had no idea what she was even saying. This was something I knew nothing about; a concept so foreign to me that I didn't even have a clue how to begin addressing it.

17 March 2010

Today I'm not feeling so calm about things again. I've never considered myself as someone who has wild mood swings, but this is insane.

God, this shitty little island is so awful. Amongst the younger locals, the men resemble sumo wrestlers, yet the women are really pretty. But with the older people, the women resemble sumo wrestlers and the men seem to have descended into toothless heaps of alcohol-ridden apathy. And they all drive so badly. They just yell at each other, competing to see who can drive the worst while throwing random shit at each other.

We've spent the day driving around, looking at crappy beaches and rubbish architecture and monuments. As if I need "culture" in my life right now. Cat is acting like nothing has happened, and her parents are oblivious to any of it. I'm burning up inside, having conflicting feelings of intense love for my wife, confusion over what's happening, hatred for this Simon fuck and, all the while, feeling stupid, betrayed, and used. I fucking hate this place. I hate everything about it, and about my shitty, complicated life. I want to be at home. Fuck that, I want to be back in my real home: Brazil. I want to be with my friends; with people I know, people who don't lie to me.

18 March 2010

I've heard about this shit. I've watched plenty of videos on the internet. I've seen so much fucked-up stuff ... People crapping on each other while wearing leather or rubber masks that cover their faces. I mean ... Really? Jesus! Where is the gentle, caring, intelligent, fun girl that I married? What the fuck, man? I feel like such an idiot. All this time, I had no clue. And I thought I was the hardcore one. Christ.

I can't live with not knowing details, so I asked Catherine to tell me a bit more about what she and Simon have been up to. Getting Catherine alone in the first place was fucking impossible, with her parents and the kids around, constantly wanting attention. Great timing on telling me this news, Cat. Seriously.

I needed an idea of what she and Simon are doing, what was getting her so fucking hot that she'd gone behind my back to get her kicks. At first she couldn't tell me. I can see why, in hindsight. But I kept asking; kept telling her I needed to understand. So after a lot of pestering, she finally told me. She said Simon had texted her with an initial "test" to see how she'd respond. Her task was to wear a dress and go into town, and, at some point, head into a bathroom, remove her panties, and put them into her handbag. Then she had to find a café, order and drink a coffee and, after that, do a bit of window shopping. That had happened a few weeks ago. I knew about none of this at the time, which is probably the most galling part of it; my life was just carrying on as usual, and I was completely trusting and unaware of her deception. I feel like a fucking idiot. Anyway, the test apparently went splendidly; Simon understood that Catherine was a willing submissive, and Catherine got some serious thrills. And I stayed at home washing dishes. Marvellous.

19 March 2010

When Catherine first told me what Simon had tasked her to do as an initial test – put her panties into her bag and walk around town – I was shocked, repulsed, confused, and angry. Yet to my surprise, the more she described this to me, and the more I thought about it, the more aroused I became. What was *that* about? Is it a sign that I could potentially get into this kink stuff, too? God knows. Right now, I can't even think beyond this betrayal.

20 March 2010

We're going home tomorrow. We've tried to retain a semblance of normality, which has been insanely difficult. Of all the times to have this happen, crammed into a villa with our children and Catherine's parents has not been ideal. The in-laws don't seem to suspect anything, although they have commented on the tension, which is *really* helpful. We keep telling them it's due to Catherine's looming deadline for her master's degree. I hope they buy it.

Although, the way I'm feeling right now, I'd love nothing more than to watch Cat having to explain all of this to them.

22 March 2010

I've seldom felt so tense and miserable. The army was a breeze in comparison. And having children didn't even come close, although at the time I seemed to think nothing else on Earth could ever prove more of a challenge. Hell, even having Tracey leave me, all those years ago, didn't feel as disempowering as this. I keep wondering if things would be any different if I was more of an alpha male; one of those testosterone-fuelled monkeys who spends weekends drinking with mates and fucking loose women in alleyways, all the while expounding their love to Wifey back home who is looking after the kids because that's what Wifeys do. I can't change who I am; I can't undo a lifetime of being taught values, of having had a decent upbringing by a mother who told me to respect women, to treat them equally but with deference. Yet women don't seem to want a man like me. They seem to desire "strong" men. If being a strong man means treating women like dirt, then I'll leave it to other, more capable males. Maybe that's what Catherine needs. But she won't get it from me. I won't stoop to that.

You love a woman with all your heart; you give her the care, attention, and respect you believe she deserves, yet still leave her enough space to feel like she's not being smothered. That's what I have always considered gentlemanly behaviour. It's a hell of a delicate balance, but I really have tried, both with Catherine, now, and with Tracey, all those years ago. And where does it get me? Pissed on. Pushed aside in favour of newer and more exciting avenues. Yet I have heard countless stories of women who are treated like absolute shit by the men they decide to pair up with, and these women spend their lives putting up with that crap, blaming themselves for the abuse inflicted upon them, and defending their lowbrow, obnoxious cavemen with all the love in their hearts. It seems pretty obvious to me what I'm doing wrong. Yet I can't change my nature or my view of women. Seems I'm doomed to failure, even as I aspire to being the perfect companion. How I love the fucked-up human psyche.

6 April 2010: a letter, unsent

Catherine, my Catherine. I can't get my head around all of this. We haven't discussed it much, recently, and I'm not really sure I want to. My head is spinning.

Cat, think about when you found out your mother was fucking around with her best friend's husband (infidelity seems to be something of a familial trend). Think about how you felt for your father, the man who was hurt the most by what happened. He loved your mother and so he stayed with her, living with that hurt, to this very day. Think about how you felt when your ex-boyfriend dumped you for someone else; someone new and exciting. Pretty shitty, no? The bitter taste of becoming second fiddle; of being cast aside in favour of something fresh. That feeling eats at you, makes you feel ill, and fills your head with all sorts of crazy thoughts. So how does it feel to be on the giving end, now? You've expressed feelings of remorse to me, feelings of regret, of guilt, of self-loathing. And yet ... it can't be all that bad, since you've continued down this path, telling yourself that it's something you have to do, something that may end up hurting the ones you love, but which would ultimately end up hurting you more if you suppressed it. You know what that sounds like? That sounds like bullshit. Selfish, indulgent bullshit. Is that about right? Oh, but hubby is a big boy, he's handled far worse situations in the army, he's shot people and blown them up and this is nothing compared to any of that awful stuff. But if he can't handle it, if he crumbles like a lightweight and leaves you, well then, that's a sacrifice you'll just have to live with. You have these urges, these cravings, and you know they're wrong, you know people will get hurt, hell, you know that you could end up destroying yourself, your career and your life, and yet .... yet you just have to do this, because it feels so damn good! Am I being too harsh? I do apologise if I'm hurting your feelings. Maybe it's because I'm feeling a little bit ... oh, I don't know ... betrayed?

Aside from everything else, how much thought have you given to what happens to us, as a family unit, if anyone finds out what you're

doing? Our friends, the home we've created in our quiet little village, our kids' schooling ... All gone. What about the rest of our family? What would you tell them? And how about the career you've worked so hard to build, rising up the ranks over the course of a decade; all that time and effort we both put in so that you could achieve your lifelong dream to teach? It seems you're willing to piss that away, all for a few cheap thrills. But I probably don't understand any of it; it's so much more complicated than that. I'm just not intellectually strong enough to conceive of the emotional vigour this activity provides you with. Oh, I'm sure you're very careful in your approach to the whole business. But you know what? Shit happens, when you least expect it to. And when it does, please don't expect me and the kids to be there waiting, holding up placards welcoming you home again. Because I just can't promise you that. Not for a second.
D

11 April 2010

I've been doing quite a bit of reading, online. Catherine hasn't been able to explain why she needs to do this with Simon. She can't tell me what she's feeling inside; just keeps saying she is unable to describe what it's all about. Which is fantastically helpful to me, obviously. From what I've read so far, Cat is a submissive. A submissive is someone who willingly submits, or gives themselves, mind, body and soul, to another person. And here I thought that's what marriage was. Tsk. Silly me. A dominant is someone who the submissive trusts with their life, and who will take control of the submissive. They will do things to the submissive, including inflicting pain and causing humiliation, which in turn grants the submissive pleasure. I absolutely do not get it. The submissive apparently derives pleasure from knowing that what they are doing is granting the dominant pleasure. This power exchange, the giving of themselves, is the turn-on, and not specifically the acts they perform. Um. OK. The dominant/submissive dynamic is referred to as D/s. A capitalised "D" and small "s" denotes the "I'm in charge" and "I'm not" thing. Honestly, that's pathetic. It's like being back in school again. But, anyway. The submissive will obey the dominant up to a point; when things become too scary, the "sub" can ask for it to stop. And the dominant will apparently obey. This is fucked up. How will they obey? If some guy has a woman strapped naked to a bed and is horny as hell, he won't put his cock inside her just because she asks him please not to? Really? I don't think so. Not in this world. Although having said that, the number of people apparently involved in this BDSM stuff reaches into the hundreds of thousands, if not millions. And, unless at least half of them are lying, maybe it does happen. I can't see how, though; something like this just screams of inviting abuse. But people from all walks of life do D/s: lawyers, doctors, judges and politicians, teachers … So maybe, who knows, just maybe, it does work like that. Like some cult thing, where members are forced to obey the rules, to follow strict guidelines. Everything I've read, so far, indicates that this is the case. There's something called "SSC", which stands for "Safe, Sane, and Consensual", that people involved in kink have to abide by. Who polices this, though? Could someone not beat the crap out of their partner and claim in court that it was just a sex game? I don't get it. Clearly, I need to read more. A lot more.

12 April 2010

After further prompting from me, Catherine told me something else that she and Simon had chatted about. I guess I should be grateful that she's being honest with me. We're kinda getting stuff out in the open right now (well, mostly she is), and I suppose it's therapeutic in a way. Although this bit of info ... wasn't. On our return trip from the airport, after that disastrous "holiday", Catherine was supposed to call the valet service when we landed, to allow them some time to get our car ready for us. As it turned out, she forgot. And so the entire family spent forty minutes waiting outside the airport, in the cold. When Catherine reported this incident to Simon, he saw it as an opportunity to "punish" her. He told her that, the next time she went to stay at a hotel, she was to take along a pair of very high-heeled shoes and a bag of wooden clothes pegs. Then she was to stand in a corner in her shoes for forty minutes, applying one new peg somewhere on her body every minute. This incident bothered me a lot, not due to the actual punishment or eroticism involved, but for the fact that details of our personal life – including mine and the children's – was acting as fuel for Simon's fantasy.

I was too gobsmacked to say anything to her right then. I just went quiet and turned over in bed. She went to sleep (takes her about three seconds, on average), while I lay there seething about the general fucking mess that my life had become.

14 April 2010: a letter, unsent

> *Cat,*
>
> *You asked me last night in bed whether I was OK and I said I was fine. But I am not fine. Not by a very long way. I've never been so miserable in my life. So I lied to you. Sorry. First lie I've ever told you; and it was actually OK. Now I know how it feels to do that. Seems it's pretty easy, eh?*
>
> *Having you lie to me was hard, but I handled it. But lying to myself is where I absolutely, definitively have to draw the line. You can't live a life without your fix, and I can't live my life with it. This is not going away, and it never will.*
>
> *I've tried; God knows how hard I've tried to accept this, to just let you have everything you want from life. I've denied my own feelings, denied my own happiness, and I can no longer do that.*
>
> *I wish I could tell you exactly what the problem is, but I can't put my finger on it. The best I can come up with is that I'm jealous; jealous that another man is the object of your sexual fantasies. That just doesn't seem right to me. Am I suddenly a traditionalist? Maybe. But*

you have relinquished your dignity for the sake of a few thrills. Which, in my mind, seems the greater sin. I'm guessing that you won't, for a second, see what you're doing as sinful. And, based on most of what I've read recently, maybe it isn't. But what you're doing to me is. Why should I have to try and be OK with this? I haven't done anything wrong, yet it's become my problem to deal with. That's just so incredibly unfair.

For the sake of our two beautiful little people, I have to stay. They have no say in this, it is not of their making, and it would be the most unfair thing I've ever done in my life to leave them. I love you with all my heart, so dearly, yet I don't like you very much, right now. And I hate that you've put us in this position.
D

20 April 2010 (Day entry)

I've had an epiphany. Having reread a previous entry, it dawned on me that maybe I *can* stoop, albeit in a mutually beneficial manner.

I've spent a large part of my day reading various websites, and then I did something that I'm hoping will save my marriage and my sanity: I composed a letter to Catherine. And this time, I actually sent it.

It went like this:

Sorry if this fucks with your working day, but I need you to read it. Don't worry; it's painless (for now). Call me when you've read it – the house is clear.

I've been doing some research. What follows are my words and my concepts. I honestly don't know what I'm doing and I don't know where to start on this adventure, but I think this letter is as good a place as any.

I was stupid and naïve to ignore your initial prompt that night, when you asked me to read the article on spanking. You reached out to me but I didn't give it any thought, or the attention it clearly deserved. There is some very nasty shit out there and I want no part of that stuff. That's what initially turned me away; a misconception of what the D/s world involved. However, having read more, I'm finally beginning to understand what you've been trying to tell me. I now know that I can provide you with what you need.

I want to explore with you, and to explore you. I want to become your Dom. The idea of doing so excites me. Perhaps "Pseudo-Dom" is more accurate at this point, but give me time – I don't have any experience, but I'm willing to learn. I want to learn, and I want to learn with you. And I don't feel weird about it, I feel excited. Believe me; I want to do this.

Given our situation and commitments as a couple and as a family, spontaneity may not always be possible. Some situations could be awkward or even dangerous, but we'll deal with them if they happen. We'll need to be careful around the children and never have them become affected by any of this, which I know is, for both of us, the most fundamental priority.

You will need to trust me completely. I won't inflict any pain on you that I'm not comfortable with, but I will play with you and together we'll discover our limits. I'm not promising results, but my mind is made up. I know you might have your doubts about this proposal, but I don't.

I won't attempt to give you exactly what you want; I will give you exactly what I want. And you will accept it. We will establish limits as we proceed.

Do you to consent to this?
D

I reread it once, and then emailed it. I knew her phone would beep with an incoming mail any second. For the next hour I shook like a leaf, trying to find things to occupy my mind.

Then I got her response: *Can't read it right now, am in a meeting.*

I'm so glad I made the effort. My timing has always been so completely and utterly fucking shite.

However, after a further four hours she responded: *I love you – thank you for trying this. Of course I trust you, completely: more than anyone else on the planet! It might feel weird, and I feel quite bewildered after a spell of emotional turmoil, but in spite of the self-consciousness and early awkwardness, I am excited by your email.*

I guess then that your word is final on it. Let's try, and see where it takes us.

Can you book a hotel room for us tonight somewhere? I'll put it onto my credit card and label the expense "marriage saving"! You are the most amazing man. This is what I wanted from the start, so if you can live with trying, I am the luckiest woman.
Cat x

The sense of relief I felt was astounding.

I immediately booked a hotel room for that evening, including a dinner arrangement. I chose Catherine's outfit: a full body stocking with open crotch and nipple areas that she'd bought a few months ago to arouse me (it did, and it left a lasting impression); a loose dress that I thought would suit the occasion, and shin-length boots. Not high heels, sadly – she doesn't own many of those. Yet.

20 April 2010 (Night entry)

At dinner, we flirted. I asked for a table that was away from the others, behind a wall, which afforded us a bit of privacy. I took my first tentative steps, asking Catherine to dip a finger into her glass of water and then rub herself under the cover of a tablecloth. At one point I lightly tugged her left nipple. The conversation was easy, and laden with innuendo. The food was great. I have absolutely no idea what we ordered.

We finished dinner, including dessert, and headed upstairs. I was incredibly turned on, and I wanted to fuck Catherine as soon as I possibly could. But this isn't "the norm" within the BDSM community, from what I've read; I needed to be completely in control of the situation. As Cat entered the room I placed my hand on her chest to stop her, and then leaned behind her to close the door, brushing across her right breast as I did so. I blindfolded her and slowly removed her dress and boots. I left her to stand there for a while, unable to watch me as I noisily emptied a pre-prepared bag of "toys" and arranged them on a chair.

I returned to her, intending to remove the body stocking, but decided instead to lead her forward, slowly, with a scarf wrapped lightly around her neck. I left her standing for a while longer – not too long, around two minutes – before removing the scarf and then the stocking. Then I wrapped her upper body in red PVC tape, pinning her arms to her sides but leaving her hands free. When Cat bought and presented the tape to me a few months back (to have some fun as and when we found a use for it, or so I had naïvely thought), I didn't initially see the point of it, or what possibilities it could offer. But now I found myself imagining that we could need a whole lot more of it in the future.

I made Catherine sit on the bed briefly, and then recline to lie on her back, sideways across the bed. It was a king-sized bed, and she fitted perfectly from edge to edge. I was delighted. I opened her legs. She moaned, and I wondered if she had any idea how hard I was at that moment. Judging by how wet she was, I guessed she probably did. I started by writing on her inner thighs with a ballpoint pen. I wrote *I am a very naughty girl*, but it was messy and illegible, because she was squirming so much. I didn't think to tell her to lie still; I was still so very new at this game. I decorated the writing with floral patterns, becoming increasingly artistic as I made my way closer to Catherine's vagina. Once my artwork was complete I placed a clothes peg on each of her nipples, and then left her. The room had an armchair, so I sat there and watched her for a while.

After that I pinched her all over her body, but gently. I had deliberately ensured that Cat still had just enough freedom to move her arms and hands sufficiently to reach her pussy. I told her to start touching herself, slowly working up and down her thighs and then to her genitals. I told her to touch softly, and ordered her not to come. After ten minutes or so I pretended to remove my trousers, and started making noises to let her think I was masturbating. I was rubbing and tapping my leg as I sat in the chair, fully clothed, watching her reactions. I told her to insert a finger into herself and to then alternate between doing that and rubbing her clitoris until she finally reached orgasm. I pretended to come, too, although I don't think she heard or even noticed me. It didn't matter.

I gave Catherine a few minutes to recover, and then I flipped her over so that she was lying with her stomach on the bed and her knees on the floor, and I fucked her. I came in about three seconds. Clearly, this was working for both of us. I untied her, and we snuggled up under the covers, falling asleep in each other's arms. At last, everything feels like it's going to be OK again.

21 April 2010

I woke up at around 6.30 a.m. Catherine was still fast asleep. I woke her half an hour later, gently stroking her hair and shoulders. When she was awake and started responding to my touch, I ordered her to lie on her back, resting her hands on her inner thighs. I told her not to touch her genitals. I made Catherine run her hands over her legs and stomach, but still no intimate touching was allowed. Five minutes later I put pegs on her nipples, and told her to masturbate. After she had reached orgasm she begged me to fuck her. I was more than happy to oblige.

We flirted throughout the morning, holding hands, kissing, and snuggling like newlyweds. I was euphoric. After lunch we returned home.

At some stage during the day Catherine went shopping. An hour after she'd left the house I texted her with instructions to find a bathroom, and to let me know when she'd done that. I allocated five minutes in which she could complete this task, but I didn't inform her of this fact. After eight minutes I still hadn't had a reply so I texted again, telling Catherine that her reward was forfeit. This was her first transgression. I later learned that she hadn't heard her phone. That's too bad. As a short term punishment she was forbidden to touch herself again until I said she could. Later in the day, when she had returned home, Cat went upstairs for an afternoon nap. Before she went to sleep I told her to remove her panties. The punishment stood: no touching allowed. I woke her later by inserting a finger into her pussy, shoving it in as far as I could, and then rubbing her clitoris. Things may have progressed further but for the fact that our boys were playing downstairs.

That evening I made Catherine give me a blow job. I stopped her before I came, and told her to touch herself. I said she had three minutes in which to come. She failed. This was her second transgression. I made her suck me again, alternating between using her mouth, her hands, or both, at my discretion. I told her to do all she possibly could to make me come, setting a time limit in my head. She failed again. This was her third transgression. I relented and gently pushed her onto her back, letting her masturbate until she came. After that she tried to pull me onto her. I told her we were done. We cuddled for a while, and then I asked her to touch me. I had planned to stop again, wanting her to believe I intended to fuck her but then getting up and dressed. Sadly (although I can't, in truth, say that I was actually very sad at all, and to hell with the rules), after a short while my willpower failed and I slid my cock into her. I came hard and it was amazing; one of the best I've ever experienced. I felt slightly angry afterwards at having given in. That was *my* first transgression but, happily, I'm not the one who gets punished. It felt great, being in charge.

22 April 2010

I woke up at 5.20 a.m. I lay there, just watching Catherine, for ages. Then I removed her panties. While she was still stirring awake I attached a peg to each of her pussy lips. I ordered her to lie still. After fifteen minutes I attached a third peg to her lower labia, sealing her pussy shut. Finally, another ten minutes or so later, I clipped a peg onto her clitoris. I did this quickly, deliberately not easing it on. Catherine gasped and arched, but said nothing. After a minute I removed all of the pegs and pulled her panties back on. We lay like spoons, me behind her, and both went back to sleep.

Later that day I told Catherine to go to the local supermarket, on some random buying quest. On my orders, she removed her panties before she left. She wore jeans so that the rough fabric could rub against her. The aim was to exploit the tenderness of her genitalia after the early morning's activity. I wasn't sure I had done enough to make her vagina feel overly sensitive or painful, but the experience could potentially still arouse her. I hid a vibrator and some lubricating gel in Catherine's bag, thinking I would tell her to use them while she was out. Shortly before she left, she opened the coat cupboard under the stairs and rummaged through her bag for a phone charger. She discovered my planted items. When she saw the vibrator, her eyes widened, and she just stood there holding it. Then Robert started coming down the stairs. There was a series of crashing noises from inside the cupboard as Cat panicked and stuffed the toy back into the bag. Even though I was slightly annoyed that she had wrecked my plan, I had to stifle a laugh. Oh dear. My idea had to be revised. When Catherine had left the area – looking slightly red and flustered – I removed the large rabbit vibe and planted a smaller one instead, making sure nobody was watching. I could have aborted the plan entirely, but I figured a downgrade was a form of mild punishment, even though her "discovery" wasn't, strictly speaking, her fault at all.

I wrote a note and gave it to Catherine before she left the house. I told her to read it when she arrived at the shopping centre. The note instructed her to head into a bathroom, insert the vibrator (a c-shaped device), switch it on at a low setting, and then leave the bathroom again and continue with the shopping. My note also said that, when she arrived back home, she was to remove the vibrator. I deliberately failed to specify whether she should switch it off at any stage. I also didn't say whether she could come or not. I was trembling slightly as I imagined Catherine reading the note and performing her duties. I awaited her report with anticipation.

At one point I got a text asking if she was allowed to come. I smiled and replied, *It's your party ...'*

Catherine arrived home a while later and went straight upstairs. We had to spend the rest of the day attempting to appear "normal" in front of the children. Doing so was incredibly difficult. Catherine sat at the dining table, checking emails, in the afternoon. I walked up behind her for a loving hug. James was playing outside and Robert was watching telly. I pinched Catherine, hard, on her inner thigh. She jumped, then immediately made it seem as if she was stretching and arching her back. Good girl. I smiled. Things were going well.

Later in the evening, when we were finally alone, I listened to Catherine's report.

The experience had been pleasurable, although when she first inserted the little vibrator it felt as if it would fall out. With no panties to help keep the device in, it was uncomfortable and kept slipping. Catherine told me she'd considered removing the vibrator, but kept it in because she had been told to. I made a mental note to reward her for that at some point. Had she come from the c-shaped device? Yes, but only after she'd returned home. So that's why she took so long upstairs…

We were done for the day. We held each other as Catherine drifted off to sleep. I stayed awake another hour, thinking about our new lives and wondering what adventures awaited us.

23 April 2010

I woke up at 5 a.m., for no discernible reason. My head was spinning. There was so much to think about, especially the potential physical, social, and psychological risks associated with what we were doing. Keeping the boys completely oblivious was at the very top of that list. What if they walked in on us one night, perhaps awoken by unfamiliar noises? What if neighbours heard the spanking sounds, the orders I barked, the ecstatic moans in the heat of a session? What if Catherine was trussed up in ropes and tape, blindfolded, with no possible way of escape, and I suffered a coronary? So much to think about.

Catherine left for work at around 6.30 a.m. I had just dropped back off to sleep, having worried about a thousand problems for which I had no answers. I woke up an hour later, when the alarm went off, and started getting the boys ready for their day. All through brushing their teeth, dressing them, and preparing breakfast, the excitement of my newfound "hobby" was foremost on my mind.

During the day I constantly checked for new emails and text messages – I couldn't care less about the trite and trivial mails from friends or family; I just kept hoping to get a few words from Catherine. Anything at all. I couldn't wait to see her again, to touch her. I felt like a teenager again, struggling to get through the day before a second date.

Knowing what I had planned for that night was troubling me, yet I was excited beyond words.

When Catherine got home from work, slightly later than anticipated, we ate and then went upstairs. The kids were, mercifully, asleep by then. I asked Catherine to trim my hair with the electric clippers, but told her she had to be naked. Once my hair was cut I told her to go into the room and prepare a range of objects. I told her to wait for me once she'd done that. She was to blindfold herself. I instructed Catherine to touch herself lightly, but not to the point of actually coming. I showered, and afterwards deliberately took my time cutting my nails and cleaning the clippers. Then I returned to the bedroom.

Catherine was lying on her back and running her hands over her thighs and breasts. I told her to stop, and lie in a spread-eagled position. I used the PVC tape and tied her hands to the small knobs at either corner of the bed. I started gently rubbing her pussy and softly explained how much I wanted to fuck her, and in which positions. I continued to play with her for a further fifteen minutes. This was exactly how long the vegetables were left to boil when she forgot about them before last night's dinner. If Simon could use our lives for inspiration, then I would sure as hell do the same.

I inserted both of my thumbs into Catherine, one in her vagina and one in her anus. Using my hands, I brought her close to climaxing, but not quite. She would be denied an orgasm today. Instead, she had to answer for being a bad girl. This "punishment and reward" concept didn't quite gel with me, but it gave me an opportunity – an excuse, even – to try different stuff. I removed my thumbs and told Catherine to lie still while I washed my hands. I returned and explained why the touching had only lasted fifteen minutes. I told her that we had to deal with a few outstanding "crimes", and I let her consider my words for a while. As she lay there, I retrieved a belt from my wardrobe. Would she prefer a paddle? A crop? I was still so new to this. I had no idea what I was doing. Everything was based on a few articles I'd read on some websites, and on what I thought could be an exciting experience for us both. As I stood there, a small part of me imagined my beautiful wife lying bruised on our bed, sobbing in pain and disappointment. In that moment I understood how easily the whole D/s dynamic could turn to abuse in the wrong hands. I didn't know if that had ever happened, but it surely must have – the world is full of fucking idiots; bullies who manipulate every situation to their own advantage. Would I become one of those people? Was I abusing a delicate situation? I had no idea. I suspected I was treading on some very thin ice.

I had to focus. I had a plan, and I needed to stick to it – my marriage and my future depended on it. I began the task at hand. I leaned in close to Catherine and began talking softly, reminding her again of her misdemeanours and the associated consequences.

Catherine's punishment would consist of one hard smack with the belt for each transgression. I didn't tell her this. I wondered if I should, but decided to keep it to myself.

Transgression number one: Catherine failed to respond to my message in time last Saturday, in which she was ordered to find a public bathroom.

Transgression number two: I had mentally allocated three minutes in which she was to masturbate and come. She failed.

Transgression number three: I asked Catherine to give me a blow job, then a hand job, and then both. She'd failed to make me come within the time limit I'd had in mind.

I asked if she accepted her punishment. If she replied yes, then the next evening's game would proceed as planned. If not, then I'd have to rethink all of the following week's events.

Cat whispered, 'Yes'. She was trembling slightly. I untied her and told her to lie on her front, arms above her head, and with her legs straight. Then I got to work.

Catherine lay on the bed, flat on her stomach, her wrists bound with rope above her head. She wore a blindfold and nothing else. She was shaking, but I had no idea if that was due to the cold or her anticipation of what I was about to inflict upon her. She was breathing fast, so I figured it was the latter. I stood at the side of the bed, studying Catherine's face. Her expression appeared calm, which was a good thing given our situation.

I had been given the thick leather belt a few years previously – by Catherine, ironically (or perhaps intentionally, who knows?) – as a Christmas present. I'd never worn it. This gift was now wrapped around my right arm. I held the belt firmly in my right hand as my arm rested at my side. I felt nervous, anxious to make a start, yet petrified because I was about to beat the hell out of the only woman I have ever loved. What were we doing? What had happened to the normal life we'd led only a few weeks ago? She wanted this, which made it OK ... Didn't it? I lifted the belt slowly, quietly, until it was poised just behind my head. Was I really going to go through with this? How was this in any way going to be a pleasant experience, for either of us?

Catherine had started to shake, a lot, and I realised, with something close to panic, that it wasn't actually very warm in the bedroom any more. Whatever I decided to do, it needed to be done quickly. I raised the belt slightly higher, inhaling in preparation for what was to come. Catherine stiffened – she must have been listening to my breathing in the silence of the room; the room where we had conceived both of our children, where we had held each other while discussing our lives, our dreams, our bright futures. I couldn't believe what was happening. It was all so surreal.

I brought the belt down with all my might, and the noise it made was deafening. Catherine's backside clenched as the blow struck. But instead of a cry of pain, she let out a moan of ecstasy. This reaction was as foreign to me as finding an elephant in my cornflakes. The feeling it stirred within me was indescribable. Exhilaration, perhaps, caused by an endorphin rush; a burst of adrenaline shooting through me in an instant. The emotional turbulence of that moment was overwhelming. It's strange, isn't it? Just when you start to think you know yourself, you discover you know nothing at all.

After I had administered Catherine's punishment, I untied her and bundled her in the duvet, holding her tight and stroking her hair. I later got up to get her a glass of water. She thanked me for her punishment as I lay down again. I held her until she fell asleep, a few minutes later.

As I lay in bed, watching this amazing woman asleep beside me, I considered what we had just done. A few things bothered me.

Firstly, the temperature. I had turned the heating up during the day, and switched on the radiator in our room. I had thought about that little detail; I hadn't wanted Catherine to be cold, or that would have ruined the experience. The room hadn't felt cold to me when I started our session. But then again, I had just enjoyed a warm shower while Catherine lay naked on the bed. I later learned that she had anticipated my return and had almost come five times. Cat had also had the foresight to cover herself with a duvet while I showered, so had stayed warm. She told me that she had felt slightly cold, but that her trembling was mainly due to being extremely turned on.

Secondly, the whipping itself. That was something I had been mentally preparing for all day. I had thought I could go through with it, but I wasn't sure. I spent a lot of the day shaking nervously and not eating or drinking, reading up on techniques, and even trying out a few practice smacks on a pillow. This form of punishment was something that I'd been seriously apprehensive about. The idea of physically beating this beautiful woman, my amazing wife and the mother of my children, with a belt (or anything, for that matter) was emotionally distressing and hugely difficult to comprehend.

As for the event itself, I had thought that three strikes would do the job. I was wrong. Catherine did seem surprised by the first stroke, but not nearly as shocked as I'd anticipated.

What I learned from the evening was that a) I was capable of inflicting some pretty serious pain upon someone I love dearly, with no psychological scarring to either of us. And b) Catherine has an incredibly high pain threshold. Three strikes had barely even begun to excite her.

24 April 2010

Catherine worked a late shift today. We flirted via text throughout the day. She arrived home tired. We ate (I had dinner ready and waiting, and the boys were already asleep) and discussed her day at work and mine at home. For all our newfound fun, real life goes on. After dinner I told her to run a bath, even though she had showered in the morning. During her bath I entered the bathroom and ordered Catherine to stand with her hands against the wall. I gently lathered her with a soft sponge, soaping every part before finishing at that magical place between her thighs. I could tell it wasn't as exciting for her as I'd have liked it to be, but I was as rigid as a post. After her bath I ordered Cat to clean the bathroom, but first I bent her over and made her wait while I fetched a prop: a butt plug that I had ordered online a few days earlier. (I had also bought a length of rope and a leather paddle which looked very much like a table tennis paddle.) She gasped briefly as I inserted the plug, but then she set about cleaning.

Once the bathroom had been cleaned, about half an hour later, I led Catherine to the bedroom and stopped her in the doorway. I blindfolded her. I grabbed her hair from behind and roughly led her to the bed, telling her to climb on, and then to get on all fours. I forced her legs open, her head facing the foot of the bed and me still behind her. I could tell she was already aroused – her pussy glistened and she was breathing heavily. I stroked her, inserting a finger once or twice, and then got out the paddle. I told her that she'd been asking too many questions and proposing too many ideas of her own. Did she think she was in charge? She had to answer for these indiscretions. I forced her to use the title "Sir" when answering me, which didn't – to my surprise – feel very awkward at all. After that, a few solid whacks with the paddle had Catherine squirming and moaning loudly, which was a huge relief for me. She sank onto her thighs a few times during the paddling. I let up for a few minutes each time, and then told her to get back up, after which I continued her punishment. She eventually fell onto her side with a loud groan.

Her arse looked like raw beef, and I felt a surge of panic. My mind was reeling. I was appalled that I had inflicted this injury on a human being who I loved and cherished more than anything on Earth. I should be holding her instead of beating her. What was I doing? And then I saw how wet she was, saw a small smile playing on her lips, and all of my tension and apprehension evaporated. I ordered Catherine back onto her knees, removed the butt plug, and fucked her hard from behind. After I was done I told her to lie on her back. She squirmed in pain as her backside rubbed the blanket. When she was lying flat I told her to touch herself. She did this to great effect, and experienced one of the strongest orgasms I've ever seen. We cuddled and talked for a while afterwards, and established that yes, this was all she'd hoped it would be. And then some.

I told her she didn't need to gather information from the internet or from books any more – that was my job from now on.

25 April 2010

Today, Catherine began a two-day training course in London. She's booked a room at a hotel nearby.

I'm toying with the idea of doing something similar to what Cat and Simon did, a while ago; Catherine standing in high heels with the butt-plug inserted, applying pegs and using a dildo or vibrator to make herself come. I like this idea, even though I'm secretly jealous that Simon was in any way a part of it. Even so, the thought is a good one, and it arouses me.

I'm thinking about emailing this idea to Catherine, but I'm wary. She could still be feeling tender from last night's activities, and may not want to experience another session so soon. I need to take some time today to think through a few ideas for getting her excited, but without too much emphasis on the physical aspect. I fear that the mental aspect of D/s will prove to be my downfall; I'm rubbish at generating ideas. I think I'll leave her to focus on her training, and save the D/s stuff for another day.

26 April 2010

9.22 a.m.
I've just dropped the boys at school and had some toast and a cup of tea. I have pretty much the whole day to myself – James is at preschool, on an all-day trial, and Robert has an afterschool French class to attend.

I'm going to spend my day putting together a string of pegs, which I will clamp, at intervals, onto various parts of Catherine's body. I'll colour-code the pegs, or number them. Then when she's lying naked on her hotel bed, at some future conference, she can call me and apply the pegs as I instruct. It's tricky, because I won't have any physical means to tell when the pain is becoming too great, so I'll have to set a time limit. Ten minutes after the final peg has been placed? Seems reasonable. I can't believe I'm just making this shit up, based on a thumb-suck estimate. It's like being some kind of virtual inquisitor, albeit a clueless one. So, after ten minutes Catherine will pull the string and all the clips will pop off, resulting in (hopefully) a most pleasant experience. After that she can insert the butt plug and touch herself until she comes. I'm considering having Catherine set up her laptop's webcam so that I can watch, but you never know who's on your internet these days. Paranoid? Hell, yes. The pictures in my head will have to do.

I like the peg idea. It's something I've seen mentioned a few times online. I wonder if people still have original ideas, or if they just reuse ideas they read about? I seem to be using up all of my tricks in very rapid succession. I'll need to find a few more. Or maybe just rework ideas I've already used. How long can I keep doing this? I'm feeling a bit knackered, if I'm honest, and haven't really spent all that much time, recently, thinking about anything else, aside from sorting out the kids and keeping the house in order. Have I made a mistake, thinking I was up to this task? Jesus, I hope not. I'll have to go back to the internet. And there I was, thinking I had a creative mind.

9.27 p.m.

Catherine and I texted on and off during the day. I told her to message me when she arrived at the hotel after her course. I'd thought of a few ideas for Cat tonight, but they all seemed trite or impractical. Finally I simply started composing a text message, instructing her to leave her underwear at the hotel while she went out to dinner at a nearby restaurant. Not original, but fun. However, before I could hit *send*, I got a call from Catherine saying she was busy having a bite to eat and then heading to the hotel. She was tired after a long day and just wanted to sleep. I hadn't relayed any instructions to her yet, so I didn't say anything about it. But my plan for tonight is now ruined. I guess that's what being a Dom is all about – thinking on your feet, changing scenarios at a whim, improvising. I've always been particularly shit at that. Catherine made it easy for me by saying an early night and a good sleep would do her good. On the plus side, at least now I have more time to come up with some new ideas. I'm trying hard not to resort to the internet. As I write this, no ideas are forthcoming. I'm not panicking yet; just slightly concerned that I may have bitten off more than I can chew.

27 April 2010

It's our one week "kink" anniversary. I can't believe it's gone by so quickly. My God, just how fast can a snake shed its skin?

Earlier in the week I'd gone online and ordered a pair of ankle-high stiletto boots and a corset for Catherine, and they arrived today. Exactly how Catherine will be wearing them, what else she'll be wearing with them (if anything at all), and various other details surrounding that scenario have yet to be worked out. I just hope that whatever I do plan doesn't turn into a case of me getting too horny and fucking her before any actual dominating takes place. I'd like to think I can control myself properly before attempting to control my sub.

I've wrapped the boots and the corset in brown paper. It is our anniversary, after all. Here's the plan: Catherine arrives home after her two days away. First, we'll get the boys to bed. Then we'll have a glass of wine and talk, probably about what she learned at her training course, although in reality all I'll be interested in is getting her naked as soon as possible. When the children are asleep we'll head upstairs. I'll stop Catherine outside the bedroom, tell her to close her eyes, and lead her into the room. The presents will be on the bed. I'll make her open the shoes first. She'll strip and then put them on. Then she'll open her second present: the corset. I'm guessing I'll be rather eager to help her to put it on ... And please, for the love of God, let it be the right size! Then I'll get undressed and lie on the bed, telling her to rub herself on me; to use my body as her come-toy. But she won't use my cock. And she won't touch herself. Will that work? Will she climax? How much time will I give her? Will I remember to put the heating on beforehand? Where the fuck can I download a decent manual on how to be a proper Dom? Hopefully, she'll come. Either way, I'll make her lie on her back, feet pulled as close to her bum as possible, and I'll blindfold her and then tie her hands behind her knees. I'll insert the butt plug, and then stroke her body with a feather, a spiky brush, a silk scarf, my hands, whatever. I'll make her wait as I go back downstairs to fetch honey. I'll drip some of the honey onto her clitoris, and then run a finger over her clit, her stomach, over her nipples, up the side of her neck and then into her mouth. After that, I'll lick the honey off her pussy. Jesus, even writing this is getting me hard.

OK, this is a good plan. Maybe at some stage I'll drip hot wax onto her from the candles I've decided to use for lighting. And I'll hope like hell I don't knock one over anywhere near a net curtain. Failure on such a grand scale is not an option here – having the fire department, police, ambulance, and the entire neighbourhood watching me try to assist her and the kids out of a burning house while she's trailing her restraints, covered in wax, and honey, and criss-crossed cane marks, is not how I plan on ending my evening.

Anyway. Best not to think about that too much. Although I do need to look into the safety aspect a bit more, some time.

Next, I'll tell Cat to raise her feet into the air, and I'll start spanking her with my open hand. If her arse is still too bruised from Tuesday night, I'll move to her upper thighs. Then I'll use the paddle, but gently, this time. Finally I'll switch to my secret weapon: a riding crop, which arrived in the mail a few days ago. God knows where the money is coming from to pay for all of these toys but, if it saves our marriage, then it doesn't really matter. Hopefully, once Cat has had enough of the spanking, she'll manage to touch herself until she comes. I really hope this works for her, or my confidence as her Dominant (or is it Dominator? God, I'm such a newbie at this) will plummet. And that will be a fucking disaster.

28 April 2010

Catherine arrived home from her course last night, utterly exhausted. We spent the evening sorting out the boys, giving them a bath, reading them stories and finally tucking them into bed. After that, we both had quick showers and then went straight to bed. We just lay there, neither of us really saying very much. There was no thought of playing, with or without toys involved; Catherine fell asleep, almost immediately.

So much for my grand schemes and detailed planning. I guess part of being a Dom is knowing when not to do or say anything.

29 April 2010

Today, I stopped shaking. Finally. I've been hyped since that first night Cat and I played at the hotel. Who knew an adrenaline rush could last so long? I've lost weight, not in any kind of "dazed inability to eat" kind of way, but simply because I haven't even thought about eating until my body demanded it, mostly late in the day or at supper time. I've realised (and so, too, I think, has Catherine) that this pace is unsustainable. While it's unbelievably wonderful, we need to live our lives. We still need to function, and even though I know we are both carrying on as close to "normal" as possible and have managed to get through our first week or so in the D/s world without any hitches on the social or personal side, I need to start thinking about the day-to-day things that I've kind of set aside. Things like worrying about finances, DIY, that kind of stuff. The mundane realities of life.

30 April 2010

It dawned on me today, slow creature that I am, that my life as it is right now could be what most teenage boys (and a few girls, too, I guess…) would consider their ultimate wet dream. Imagine conjuring up a scenario which incorporates some of your wildest sexual fantasies, and knowing that your vision will shortly play out almost exactly as you want it to. You can make your partner wear what you want them to wear. You can make them do what you want them to do. If you want to masturbate on your sub's face as they kneel on all fours in front of you, you can do it. If you want a blow job while slapping their arse, just order them to do it. How has this way of life escaped the attention of so many millions of people for so long? How was I so ignorant as to almost miss this opportunity to discover what has, for me, become a life-changing experience? The D/s dynamic is an absolute win/win situation; the perfect release for any and all sexual tension. The more I think about it, the more panicked I feel about the fact that I came so close to losing my marriage and my new, revitalised way of seeing the world, due to sheer ignorance.

1 May 2010

9.18 a.m.
It's so difficult getting this right. I imagine it's very different for single people, who can pick up play partners at will, but I feel a massive pressure to succeed at this with the woman I love. If I do something wrong, or even if I don't quite get it right, will she tell me? Because of the D/s dynamic, probably not. Although, since we usually do a situational analysis after each session (does that take away a bit of the excitement and intrigue, I wonder?), she possibly would say something at this stage. I certainly hope so. I can't fuck this up. I just can't. I need to read more, or just sit and stare into space for a

few hours and come up with a few ideas of my own. Time is a bitch. There just ain't enough of it to go around.

11.24 p.m.

We played again tonight. I included the corset and the boots. It all went as planned, pretty much. No fires, no major catastrophes. I think the anticipation of it worked best for Catherine, since I'd told her just after breakfast that we would be having a scene this evening. I decided that the bedroom was too small for what I wanted to do, so we used the living room instead.

Catherine loved the stilettos but could hardly stand in them. The corset fitted perfectly. I had to secure it at the back and doing so while Catherine was only wearing her new boots was driving me insane. I'd never thought I could ejaculate without some form of physical stimulation before now, but I very nearly did just that. Once the corset was fastened I blindfolded her. And then Catherine just stood there, arms at her side, breathing heavily, and I noticed just how wet her pussy was. A single large, glistening drop of juice hung from her. I'd never seen that before and I was so turned on that if she had asked me to, I would have fucked her there and then. It was one of the hardest mental tests I've ever had to endure, stopping myself from doing that, when I knew that I could. It's what I wanted to do more than anything, but I knew that whatever I did next was crucially important to our developing relationship as Dominant and submissive. I used every bit of willpower to breathe evenly and calm myself down. I told Catherine she had to thank me for her presents. She started giving me a blow job, but I had to stop her – I was just too damn close to coming, and I didn't want that, just yet. I told her to lie down, on a blanket that I'd put on the floor, and then I went into the kitchen to fetch the ice and the honey.

The ice idea was something I'd found on the internet; I created an ice lolly by placing a condom inside a cardboard tube from an empty kitchen roll. Then I secured the condom to the top of the tube with some elastic bands, filled it with tap water, and placed it upright in the freezer overnight. It made a really good phallus. I kept the condom on it, knotting the end to make sure it didn't slip off. After washing my home-made dildo very briefly in tepid water I covered it with lubricant and inserted it slowly into Catherine's pussy. The ice lolly apparently worked well, according to post-play analysis. Catherine suggested I use it for longer, but with more frequent breaks in between. She enjoyed the honey experience, too, which ended up as a sticky mess all over her stomach and thighs. I obviously used a bit too much, and licking so much of the sweet goop off her made me feel ill. I had decided not to use any melted wax this time. I need to avoid using up too many tricks in a single session.

I ended the scene with a spanking. I used a shatterproof plastic ruler to slap Catherine's pussy. She had mentioned the idea to me a while ago. I snapped the ruler down quite hard. Sadly, I wasn't too sure about how much pressure or strength to apply, and my heavy-handedness was too much, too hard, too intense. What Catherine had actually wanted was a slow build-up; more slaps, but softer, gradually creating a warm throbbing sensation (as opposed to my short, lightning-sharp shocks). The slaps I applied with my hand after that were equally erratic. I hadn't realised how much pain an open hand could inflict.

The most important thing we got from the evening was the realisation (for us both) that with any session involving pain, I need to let Catherine know beforehand what to expect so that she can mentally prepare for it. Random slapping and beating until your sub collapses isn't much of a turn-on, apparently. Overall, though, this was a pleasant evening with some harsh lessons learned. Oh, and I've decided that Catherine takes far too long to reach an orgasm – probably because she's doing it too often, the dirty girl. I'm imposing a one-week ban on her coming. Let's see how long that lasts, shall we? I'm guessing not very long at all.

2 May 2010

I'm so tired today. I spent a lot of last night, after Cat had fallen asleep, thinking about her contact with Simon. I'm nervous, and I'm a mess just thinking about it. I can't say why, but I still feel jealous and insecure every time I think about him being a part of her life. I spoke to Catherine about this a few days ago, and she told me that she was still in touch with Simon. The D/s situation with him isn't as full on as it had been before she and I started playing (isn't as full on? I thought they'd stopped communicating completely, for fuck's sake!). Apparently he's still emailing and texting her, and not always with kink-related content. Well, that's brilliant, then. I told Cat I wasn't entirely comfortable with the situation.

After an emotional morning of discussion – we sat in the park while the kids played, and thank fuck it was a warm day – Catherine has decided to call it off completely with Simon; no more contact at all. I'm hugely relieved. She has no idea how this is tearing me up inside. Catherine emailed Simon. She showed me the mail, and I'm grateful for that. She told him that she can no longer be in contact with him. I'm hoping that now we can carry on with our lives and leave all the bullshit behind. We were both emotionally drained after our talk and the tough decision that she had to make, so Catherine asked me for a purely vanilla day. I went out shopping with the boys while Catherine caught up on much-needed sleep.

We agreed that we're exploring this together; that the journey doesn't have to be all mine to make. Becoming a Dom is an insanely difficult job and, with nothing to go on, I'm in the dark. Yes, there are ideas all over the internet, and in books, but I don't yet know what works for Catherine, specifically. I'm learning slowly, but I need guidance. So we're creating an ideas book, where she'll write down everything that turns her on, as well as things that she'd consider punishments, with varying ratings of severity. It's a great idea – all hers, of course. We'll hopefully work our way through this eventually. I wasn't aware that I'd be capable of doing anything like this a month ago, much less that I'd want to. But now that I am doing it, and because so much is at stake, I intend to become as good at it as I possibly can. I will please my sub. I will make her beg for more. This is my task. It will take time, though. And time, as I've said countless times before ... well, time is a motherfucker.

3 May 2010

Flexibility is a key element to our D/s dynamic, it seems. We had decided not to play tonight, just to sort of let things cool down a little. So, after dinner, we thought we'd relax with a bottle of wine, and maybe watch a DVD. We had purchased *9½ Weeks* a while ago as a naughty treat to watch together, but we hadn't got around to it, due to the chaos of our lives for the past few months. So we thought that now would be the perfect opportunity to watch it. We almost even made it through to the end, but for the fact that we were both becoming ridiculously turned on. We had a blanket over us, and I was innocently resting my hand on Catherine's knee. Things escalated when I started moving my hand, and she began responding. And, of course, it ended up with my hand rubbing her on the outside of her pants. Eventually, we abandoned the film.

I told Catherine to get her trousers and pants off, and we sat on the sofa for a few minutes longer while I touched her. Then I got onto my knees under the blanket and licked her; her feet, her legs, her stomach ... and finally her pussy. Catherine was pretty wet, by then, and she tasted delicious. I had forbidden her from coming and I was hoping she'd remembered the ban. So I licked her and used my fingers on her and in her. She was a good girl and remembered that she wasn't allowed to come but, after a few minutes of me shoving my fingers into her dripping cunt, she started begging. So I relented, telling her that I'd allow it, but that she'd have to face the consequences later. She reached orgasm very quickly after that, and I told Cat that since she'd broken the ban anyway, she may as well keep going. She used her hands to touch herself, and she soon came again. Then I decided it was my turn. I ordered Catherine to sit on top of me and ride me hard as I pulled her nipples and playfully slapped the sides of her arse. She was amazing and, after we had both collapsed in an exhausted heap, I felt something like calm settling over me for the first time in weeks.

I'm going to be OK with this. Adding some spice to our lives isn't a bad thing; we're both a lot more energised and turned on than we have been in years. We've discovered a new world, and we can explore it to our hearts' content. Together. As a team. And no more Simon to contend with. Things are starting to look good again, and suddenly life doesn't suck so much.

4 May 2010

Something I touched on before; according to various articles that I've read, it seems to me that a lot of people who are into BDSM have trouble defining exactly what it is that turns them on, mentally, about the dynamic. The physical side is easy: talk dirty, play dirty. Role-playing is fun and exciting, but it doesn't explain what people are thinking while they play; it doesn't explore the very deep psychological aspect of the game. Having been Mister Vanilla for my entire life – right up until less than two weeks ago – I can honestly tell you that people who don't get it .... just don't get it. No matter what you tell them. Catherine had huge difficulty trying to find the words to explain what she was going through, attempting to understand her own thought processes and feelings, while she was taking her first dubious steps into this alternative world. I feel like an absolute bastard, having made that journey so miserable for her with all my questions and probing, in what should have been a fun, magical, and exciting time for her. But at least we seem to have resolved that, and have now started discovering what we both enjoy about it.

Even so, it's tricky to put into words what the turn-on is all about. I think that our emotional selves are buried so deeply within primal instincts; that it's more of a reaction than an emotion. We react to stimuli; we revert to our most basic, beast-like tendencies. It's all just mind games. Hormones and lust and desire – all the good stuff that religion is so desperately keen to steer us away from. And how many true BDSM devotees are twisted, evil people with plans to wreak havoc and anarchy on a global scale? Probably very few. Fewer, I'd wager, than in normal, respectable society where individuals can sit hidden behind the safe façade of their religious texts written millennia ago by anonymous monks. But I digress. Let's get back to the point.

BDSM, the alternative lifestyle, is something that most "vanilla" folk find impossible to embrace. If you're a pretty average person looking at a BDSM website for the first time, then you'll probably start noticing a few trends. For instance, some male newcomers to the scene seem to think it's incredibly attractive to others if their profile picture is a photo of their hand wrapped around their own cock. That says a lot about the person, really. Sad, deluded, and immature, for the most part. I'm not saying I'm an intellectual giant; far from it. But I can hold a polite conversation, and I'm pretty good at gauging the reactions of others. All of which makes me hopeful that taking on the role of a Dominant might just work out for me in the long term. Because, God knows, I'm in it now, and I know things about myself that I was oblivious to just a short time ago. Cat, with her revelation, has opened up a Pandora's Box, and new, exciting (and at times, terrifying) things have been flowing out of it, and into my head, ever since. And now, nothing can ever take that knowledge away from me.

5 May 2010

I have a plan. I'm hauling out the rope tonight. I'm going to tie Cat up and clamp her body with clothes pegs; twenty of the little buggers. She will stay like that for half an hour. If she manages to do so without any complaints, then she will be allowed to touch herself to orgasm. If I hear a peep, even as I remove the pegs, then further punishments will be imposed.

6 May 2010

Catherine didn't make a sound last night. I'm impressed. She writhed a bit, and opened her mouth when I removed the pegs on her labia, and I fully expected to hear her whimper, but ... nothing. I allowed her to play with herself, and it didn't take very long before she had a really intense orgasm. Not surprising; she was lying in a pool of her own wetness before she'd even begun.

13 May 2010

Aside from the assertion that D/s is empowering to subs (I refer to women, since I admittedly know nothing about male subs), I still wonder about the levels of violence involved. Yes, playing within the world of BDSM is generally consensual, bound by strict guidelines on safety, and there's a "safe word" that subs can use when it all gets too much. Which is all good and well, and consensual it may be, but it's still an act of violence against another human being. Isn't it? The feminist movement has for so long tried to raise the profile of women, to the point where women are now – for the most part, and only in civilised societies – given equal rights to men. In our western world, women are by and large no longer merely seen as playthings for men, or existing only in order to serve a man's needs. So what does D/s do for their cause? Female subs practising BDSM generally argue that it is they who are holding the reins; they who are ultimately in control of the scene they're enjoying. But, to outsiders, I imagine this concept could be hugely difficult to comprehend. This is something I'm quite interested in, especially since Catherine is a feminist herself. She assures me that she's in charge during every session. Yet, when I picture her on her knees, bound and gagged, and being beaten with a riding crop, I hardly imagine a feminist group nodding sagely and agreeing that the woman is obviously in control. I'd be rich if I could harness the power generated by Emmeline Pankhurst spinning in her grave.

18 May 2010

A night of rest was needed after a few hard sessions.

I'd planned for us to play happy families for a few days, if not weeks, just to start relaxing about the D/s stuff and starting to incorporate it into our lives without it dominating (ahem) everything else. I want us to appear, for all purposes, like everyone else within the vanilla world around us. Which is ironic, since I've always despised the image of the "ideal family" with their perfect white teeth, cute puppy, and white picket fence that is presented to the world by corporate-sponsored media. Does that perfect nuclear family even exist?

Aside from all that, the evening didn't go as planned. They seldom do. After dropping the boys off at school this morning, I texted Catherine, telling her that I thought we needed a quiet evening. However, I told her that if she left work feeling like she desperately needed a release, she should hand me her panties as she arrived home. She arrived home later than expected, as always, and, with a very tired smile, told me she wasn't really in the mood for anything. Which is what we'd agreed upon, so I was absolutely fine with that decision. While I cooked the kids' dinner, we talked in the kitchen. Robert and James were playing outside and we could hear them laughing and having fun. I decided to check Cat's marks from the previous night. So, with her standing near the kitchen doorway watching and listening for the boys coming back inside, I pulled down her pants and trousers and started softly prodding her backside. That, of course, turned me on, and I wondered if stroking her amazing arse was turning Catherine on at all. Probably not; I was realising it took a hell of a lot to get her properly wet. After a quick look, I dressed her again.

Once the kids had eaten dinner and we'd spent some time together – all of us rolling about on the living room carpet, me being the daddy bear and tickling naughty baby bears – we bathed the boys and put them to bed, and then ate our meal. Afterwards, we sat down in front of the telly with a glass of wine each; our evening winding-down ritual. After about half an hour, and entirely on impulse, I suddenly stood up and switched off the programme we were watching. I told Catherine to strip to her pants and lean over a dining room chair, with her hands resting on the top of it. She did so without hesitation. I stroked her back and her bum, and then started softly hitting her arse with the plastic ruler which was on a shelf in the corner of the room. I smacked her inner thighs and her breasts, hard enough for her to squirm a bit, but not hard enough to leave marks. Twice in two days for a beginner just seems like I'm desperate to please (which, of course, I am, but anyway ...). After the ruler paddling (or whatever it's called), I sat on the chair and made Catherine straddle me. Then I ordered her to touch herself until she reached orgasm.

After that it was my turn to be inside her. We both came. After recovering from that, we headed upstairs. Cat had a bath and I lay on the bed, reflecting on what had just happened. The D/s element had obviously been present, but the whole episode felt somehow contrived and trite, lacking any real thought or purpose. It left me feeling anxious about whether I would be able to sustain this for the rest of our lives. If I can't even make it work for a month, we're doomed. I'm starting to feel a bit freaked out that I've plunged head-first into something I know so very little about.

19 May 2010

It's not all fun; it's bloody hard work for the most part. The moment Catherine found a name for her need, when she identified exactly what it was she was feeling inside and what had been eating away at her core, at that very moment, that's when she became a nymphomaniac. One orgasm a month is no longer an option. Hell, one orgasm a *night* is seldom sufficient. Suddenly, she needs to receive input – not only physical, but in the form of flirting texts and emails – all day, every day. I'm guessing the same is true for most people who suddenly discover they're submissive (or a "real" Dominant, too, I guess), just as soon as they start to play. As a Dom, playing with your own sub in this brave new world, you'd better be bloody sure you know what you're taking on, or it could end up destroying you. It could end up destroying both of you.

21 May 2010

We've had a few quiet, non-kink nights recently. I think we both needed a break. We've watched a lot of crap on TV, spent good time with the kids, and had a lot of opportunity to just sit and talk through stuff. Cat and I both seem to be settling into this new way of living, which is slowly starting to feel more normal now that we've started taking it slower. Cat seems happy with my efforts, and I am, of course, happy that I am able to please her. I'm wondering for how long, though. This doesn't feel natural to me. It doesn't feel like something that's inside me, as it is within Cat. Even though I get turned on and enjoy many of the aspects of D/s, I keep wondering if I can sustain my interest. If I start getting bored, then Cat will pick up on that, and the dynamic will be in real danger of falling apart. And if that happens, then she will need that input from other sources. And having lived it now, physically, she will need to interact with other people to get that fix. So I have to make it work, which is worrying in itself, because this is all starting to feel like a big deal. If I have to make an effort, it's no longer fun. And if it's no longer fun, then how can I continue doing it? Fucked if I do, fucked if I don't. God, why does life always have to be so complicated?

22 May 2010

A few weeks after the whole "revealing" happened, Catherine had started making notes. She'd bought a little notepad, and made brief annotations as and when something occurred to her. She left them in my bedside drawer and asked me to read them when I wanted to and, if I had any interest, to perform the actions she'd suggested. One day while she was at work I did read them, and I remember thinking that a few of the suggestions sounded quite interesting. Others made no sense at all. For the most part the suggestions were pretty tame (based on what I now know), and included things like, *Make me write lines explaining why I forgot to put my clothes in the basket*, and, *Force me to sit still for an hour on a dining-room chair whilst blindfolded.* Fairly innocuous, I suppose, and completely meaningless to me without any sort of context or BDSM-related insight. I set the notes aside and forgot about them. In hindsight, I really should have paid more attention.

The original set of notes has been discarded, but once we started down our D/s path we decided to revive them. Catherine and I both wrote notes this time. This is a selection:

Catherine's notes

1. I'm given a number of lines to write within a set time, the lines stating what punishment I deserve, followed by you inflicting the punishment on me. Increased punishment for lines not completed in time, errors, bad spelling, etc.

2. I'm told I will be punished with a number of strokes, but I have to stand facing the wall or a corner – still and silent – for the same number of minutes first. Increased time and/or strokes for moving or making a noise.

My notes

1. You strip. Then put on your stiletto boots. Insert the butt plug. Next, sink onto your haunches, with your back against a wall. Run your hands all over your body, but don't touch your pussy.

To self: the aim is to test endurance (squatting) and willpower (not touching).

2. I tie you to a chair and clamp your nipples. Your legs are spread and tightly bound. I apply lashings with a crop across your upper thighs and breasts.

3. I rub ice cubes all over your naked body, not getting to your pussy until every other inch of you has been addressed. I take my time with the ice on your clitoris. Afterwards I touch and lick you to warm you up.

4. You're on your knees on the bed, blindfolded. I bind you elaborately, and clamp you with pegs; nineteen in total, all attached with a piece of string. The final peg is applied to your clitoris. You will lie there quietly. After a while I'll yank them off you with one sharp tug.

To self: 15-minute time limit.

[This is an idea I read about and may have mentioned previously. Still seems like a good one to me.]

5. You lie on the bed on your front, with your bum in the air and arms at your sides. I bind your wrists to your ankles, and then insert the butt plug into you. I keep you waiting in that position and when I think you're least expecting it, I'll start spanking you with the paddle.

6. I'll wait for a day when you're out at the shops or having a coffee. I want you to take a photo of your pussy on your mobile phone, and send it to me.

7. You're wearing your pants and nothing else. I sit on a dining-room chair and draw you across my knees. I spank you with my bare hand through your panties. After thirty strokes on each cheek I stop and we both rest. Then I pull down your pants and spank your bare bum; another thirty strokes on each cheek.

So far we've used ideas 2, 3, 4 and 5. They were all a roaring success. I can't wait to try the rest.

23 May 2010

Unfortunately, BDSM is not something that can easily be discussed down at your local pub. Imagine meeting Bob for a beer and him telling you about his day. 'So, what about you?' he asks, ending the banal and tedious recount of his day at the office which included such highlights as sitting behind a desk, ordering a baguette for lunch, and smashing numbers onto a spreadsheet. And I answer, 'Well, Bob, I did some housework, fetched the kids from school, bathed them, fed them, put them to bed. Then Catherine came home and I beat the crap out of her, forced her to blow me, and went to sleep content in the knowledge that I can look forward to this happening for the rest of my life.' Cue awkward silence, save for the sound of glasses being dropped and police sirens. I'd love to be able to speak to someone about all of this, aside from Catherine, of course. I'm not really sure how any of my friends would handle the news. Probably best not to say anything.

25 May 2010

I spent my morning at a toddlers' group with a bunch of mums. They all sat and chatted and ignored me for the most part – as always. Except that today, that's exactly what I wanted. I was busy with my new notepad, devising ideas and schemes. I became aroused a few times, but because I was on a chair in the corner on my own and didn't move, I don't think anyone noticed. And if they did? Well, I couldn't really care less.

Here's what I've written so far:

My list of "Punishments": the five levels of severity

Level 1
Clamps
Light spanking (bottom) with hands
Binding (PVC tape)
Level 2
Clamps
Light spanking (bottom/body) with hands and paddle
Binding (restraints)
Level 3
Butt plug
Moderate spanking (body, pussy) with a ruler/brush
Binding (rope)
Level 4

Clamps and butt plug
Hard spanking (bottom) with a paddle and brush
Binding (rope)
Level 5
Hard spanking (full body) with a crop
Binding (restraints)
Gag
Boots

God. If the mums in this group had any idea what I was furtively scribbling in my little book ... I wonder if that knowledge would make any of them more attracted to me, or would they run away screaming? It's an interesting, and somewhat arousing, thought.

So, what will I do with Catherine, tonight? What would I like to do? I need to sit and think about that for a bit. Oh, the possibilities ...

26 May 2010

As it turned out, we did nothing. Catherine started her period yesterday. So now what the fuck do I do?

I've become such a potty-mouth, like I was 23 again. Every second word is "fuck". I've lost my ability to think, it seems. I've reverted back to caveman mode, which is something I hate. I used to pride myself on the fact that I was unlike so many other men; that I could control my anger; that I wasn't drawn to sports, and beer, and red meat like some primitive, chest-beating Neanderthal. Yet here I am, cursing and beating up my wife. Progress comes at a price, it seems.

So, the period thing. Tricky. I can't be dominant if she's not in the mood. She feels "unsexy and fat'" when she's having her period, apparently. OK. I tell her to let me know when it's over. I have no idea how the threat of upcoming punishment – which is what turns Catherine on about the D/s dynamic – will operate when she feels unsexy, but let's see how this works out. The way hormones mess with women having their period, I could be the one who ends up with his pants down and receiving a sound beating.

27 May 2010

OK, enough with the rhetoric. I'm starting to bore myself. The spontaneity and absolute buzz of the past few weeks is starting to wear off, and I'm miserably coming to realise that I'm the same dull and vapid creature I always was. Thing is, the more I get into the D/s stuff, the more creative I feel. Weird. The fact that I have to think about what kinds of pain and pleasure to inflict upon my unsuspecting wife seems to be forcing my brain to wake up after a very long hibernation.

So, what will we get up to tonight? I believe Catherine's period isn't bothering her too much. She has a coil inserted as a contraceptive device, and she tells me her periods don't last too long, which is handy. I had planned to spend the day outdoors, fashioning a wooden paddle from a plank I found in the garage. As it turns out, it's pissing rain outside. I can't work in the garage, because the clothes horse is in there, and I'd get into trouble if all the delicates were covered in dust.

Edit one: I've found another piece of wood that's perfect for a paddle. Since I can't fashion it into a proper paddle (i.e. cut and shape a handle), I'll just use it as is. There you go – the evening's entertainment is sorted. I haven't put Catherine over my knee yet for a proper spanking. Tonight may be just the night for it.

Edit two: The paddle worked! Cat loved it. She had bought a few pairs of stockings (fishnets, of all things) the previous weekend, and I made her try them on for me. She had also (naughty girl!) bought an object called a "bullet", which is basically a small vibrator designed for clitoral stimulation. And she's already used it! Without so much as a "by your leave, Sir". I'm making a note of all her misdemeanours, in order to allocate punishment. Anyway, she put on her stockings, but nothing else. I got an instant hard-on the moment I entered the bedroom. I sat on the bed and told Cat to suck my cock, which she did. It was an amazing blow job, but I stopped her before I came. Then I told her to kneel beside me, pulled her over my lap, and spanked her with the paddle. She became incredibly wet, and I told her to show me how her bullet worked. She demonstrated, and begged me to allow her to climax, which I did. She came hard. Then she climbed onto me and rode me until I came. I hadn't told her to do that, but quite frankly I didn't care. It felt incredible.

29 May 2010

Every now and again a small and sane part of me kicks in and I think, 'What the fuck am I doing?' I consider this amazing woman who I married all those years ago; we've had two children, and we've built a life together. Yet here I am, treating her like shit, beating her, humiliating her ... Christ, what a head trip. What we're doing can't be normal. But what is normal, exactly? Doing what the rest of the world expects us to do? A logical order of things, as dictated by our ancestors and fed down through the generations? So we're never allowed to acknowledge that, deep down inside, we're all just beasts who want nothing more than to rut in a muddy pool of our own filth? Bullshit.

How do you go back to "normal" after discovering something like this? It's impossible. It's like unseeing a horrific traffic accident. Last night I had a beautiful woman dress up for me in five-inch heels, a tight black corset, a blindfold, and nothing else. I cannot begin to think for a second that reverting back to vanilla is even an option. This is a fantasy; it's most men's wildest sexual wonderland presented on a platter. Catherine told me she couldn't describe her attraction to the D/s dynamic, and I couldn't understand why it was so difficult to explain. Only now am I beginning to understand that draw, the adrenaline rush, the intense sexual arousal that BDSM play elicits.

30 May 2010
Catherine had a lie-in this morning, in preparation for

a late night of study. After she got up, and since Robert was at school, we fetched James from preschool and took him along with us to a café for lunch. As always, the child was a beacon of social brilliance at the sandwich bar. He only screamed a few times, and ran around bashing into other people's tables once or twice. I do so love taking him out in public. When we got home again I put James in his cot for an afternoon nap.

Catherine had wanted to spend some time in her study, or at the coffee shop, to do some work on her CV. I ordered her upstairs, instead, pulling down her knickers as she went. I made her lie down and play with herself, stopping her before she came. (I've since discovered that this practice is called "edging".) I hauled out my new, home-made paddle and gave her four sets of smacks on various areas of her upper thighs and bottom, and then told her to continue masturbating. She came quickly after that. I loved watching her. I also enjoyed the fact that I had managed to orchestrate a brief (and unplanned) bit of fun. I'm starting to feel like I'm more in control of events. I think that's a positive sign that things are working. I really hope Catherine feels the same way. She's assured me that what I'm doing is working for her, but I still occasionally catch a look in her eye that leaves me feeling uncertain. And she also still mentions Simon now and again; mostly with reference to some of the things the two of them talked about when they were flirting. I should be grateful to him, for helping Cat out when she needed it the most, and, therefore, helping us find our way to where we are now. He could have been an utter wanker and hurt her emotionally, but apparently he was a complete gentleman. Be that as it may, I still want to punch him in the face. The cheeky twat.

1 June 2010

I seem to be slacking. No fresh ideas for a while now. But earlier, as if by coincidence, Catherine presented me with a little wrapped parcel before she left for work. She told me to open it after the boys had been dropped off at school.

Inside the box was a game – a beginner's introduction to BDSM.

I spent a while looking through the various "instruction" cards, and imagining Cat and I playing. After a quick browse, I decided the game was best investigated with a partner, so I put it in the bedside drawer and turned on the telly.

5 June 2010

The past few days have been busy. Catherine has had various bits of admin and a presentation to prepare, so has stayed late at work and been out at the library for some of the weekend. I understand that she has to do the work, but explaining to the children why Mummy is at home so infrequently is heartbreaking. Cat feels guilty as hell, but she's the working parent and her job security dictates the stability of our future. Maybe I should start looking for work again. Would I be able to face wearing a suit every day, and pandering to the pathetic egos of senior management, when what

I'd really prefer to do is kick them in their smug, arrogant faces? It's a dilemma. I need to think about that for a while.

7 June 2010

Catherine worked late yesterday. More toil for her, more solitude for me.

She wore a skirt to work today. Sometimes, I actually do notice details. At one stage during the morning I felt horny, but wasn't really in the mood to masturbate. I texted Cat, telling her to remove her knickers before getting home.

When she arrived home we went out for coffee at a local garden centre. Afterwards I told her to take her bullet vibe to the bathroom, and use it to make herself orgasm. She did as I told her, but she didn't come. I was slightly frustrated, and not really sure whether this counted as her wilfully disobeying me and therefore requiring punishment.

After dinner this evening, I asked Cat if she needed an early night. She told me she should be OK for a while longer, so we opened the BDSM game to see what it was all about. The game was disappointing, and not very exciting at all. It blurred the Dom and sub roles; half the cards instructed "she" to do various things to "he", and vice versa. I guess if we were newlyweds wanting to have some fun (or if we were perhaps slightly inebriated, which is strongly advised against in BDSM etiquette) it would have been more appropriate. As it was, I chose one "topping" card, which required her to touch me all over as I lay blindfolded. I didn't get blindfolded, though – that would have been taking the role reversal thing a bit too far, I thought. The rest of the "she to he" cards were binned, as were most of the "he to she" ones, although I did keep a handful of them which I thought could be fun to try at some point. Cat touched me for a while, as instructed by the card, but we both got bored with that pretty quickly. Soon afterwards she went to sleep and I sat down to write this. I suspect the BDSM game was perhaps designed by people who don't know very much about kink at all. People like me. People who should probably stay the fuck away from it.

8 June 2010

Catherine disappointed me, yesterday. I gave her a simple task, when we went to the garden centre for coffee; to head into the bathroom and make herself come with a device specifically designed to make women orgasm. It's not that hard. Yet she couldn't do it. Is it me? Am I not being forceful enough? I'd like to think that's not the case, and that she was just tired. Or, maybe, she's just come too much lately.

Tonight, we'll work on patience again. Cat will wear her blindfold, fishnet stockings, and stiletto boots. Nothing else. I'll tie her hands behind her as she stands in a corner, facing away from me, and I'll place pegs all over her breasts and a few other places on her body. I forgot to mention that there was one other, potentially interesting, item in our highly shit BDSM game: a tiny rubber flogger. I kept that, even though I have no idea what to do with it. Maybe I'll find out later.

9 June 2010

Cat just texted me her log. Good girl. Last week I'd asked her to start keeping a list of transgressions and confessions. This needs to be done on a weekly basis. It should give me something to work with when I'm considering punishments and rewards. The entries don't need to be prolific. They should, instead, consist of small things that Cat forgot to do, or any mistakes or accidents which occurred during the day. She's an incredibly efficient person, so she doesn't often fuck up. Add to that the fact that I hardly ever see her, and finding faults is tricky. It should be useful, having her help me. Maybe she'll even get a kick from it, too. It's all part of the game.

Catherine's log consists of transgressions from the past month and more; it's a first attempt, something new for us both. It reads as follows:

> ***Transgressions***
> *1. Impatient with instructions at the shops.*
> *2. Asked to come but failed despite being told there would be consequences.*
> *3. Did minimal work on the weekend.*
> *4. Forgot to phone you when I got to the shops – I was already inside when I remembered.*

OK, let's see. First one ... I can't remember. Hell, I'll punish her anyway. Second: interesting that she used the phrase "asked to come", thereby, probably, implying that I should have ordered her to do so instead. Is she being impertinent, or just confused?

Whose fault is that one, then? Not sure that I can rightfully punish her for it. Thirdly, yes, she did minimal work. But that's because she spent much-needed time with her family, and wanted a small amount of quiet time to herself after yet another shitty week at work. Does that deserve punishment? Christ, this list isn't helping at all. And finally, yes, she did forget to call. It was a while ago, but I'll use it. It's a minor transgression, but at least we have one concrete thing to work with. I'll be administering this punishment using the pegs and the flimsy little rubber flogger that came with the BDSM game, and which I was planning to use at some point anyway. I have a proper reason to do so now.

10 June 2010

Last night was a success. I think. Once the kids were asleep I told Cat to go upstairs and get undressed, then put on her fishnet stockings, stilettos, and blindfold. I gave her five minutes to do this while I prepared a glass of water for each of us. When I got upstairs she was ready, standing still at the foot of the bed with her arms at her side. I became aroused immediately. The vanilla part of me wanted to throw her onto the bed and fuck her right then – which I guess could have worked as a "rough play" idea – but I resisted. I've always had pretty good willpower; without it I probably would have ended up being incarcerated years ago for punching some cunt in the face for doing something irritating. However, employing that willpower right now was incredibly difficult. But it had to be done, in order for this to work.

I ran a finger from just under Cat's chin to just above her clitoris, and held it there. She shuddered when I stopped. Then I got out the packet of pegs from my goodie bag. I really must remember to buy more of them; half of our washing ends up blowing away on windy days. I clamped one peg onto each nipple, and three more around the curve of each breast. I followed up with three pegs on the inside of each thigh, ending with two pegs on each of her outer lips. I ordered Cat to turn and face the corner, and walk forward a few paces. I had to steady her a few times; she's not used to wearing very high heels. If she had fallen with the pegs attached, the moment (and, quite possibly, a few bits of important anatomy) could have been damaged. Vigilance, it would seem, is massively important when playing with someone.

When she reached the corner, I told Cat to place one hand on each of the walls to her sides. Then I made her squat and hold the position. I'd been forced to squat in the army, holding a rifle out in front of me horizontally, with both arms stretched out. I lasted about three minutes. I was hoping Cat could do better, and she did; ten minutes later, I helped her to stand. She hadn't made a sound, and simply exhaled when she stood. I helped her to the bed, where she climbed on and knelt. I slapped her backside ten times on each cheek with my bare hands, and then ten times again with the flogger. It's a pathetic little device, and after the session it went into the bin. Mental note: I need to order something more substantial online. Cat hadn't responded to the flogger at all, but seemed to enjoy the spanking. After the miserable flogging attempt I couldn't hold out any longer, so I inserted my cock into her. I realise that Catherine's needs outweigh mine, and I really should have tried to play with her for a bit longer. But I'm new at this and, anyway, she didn't object. After I had come, I turned her over and removed all the pegs, then touched her until she reached orgasm. She later confirmed that she would have enjoyed a bit more spanking, and also a while longer to savour the moment immediately after I had removed the pegs, before I'd entered her. My mental notebook is filling up rapidly.

18 June 2010

It seems like time is flying by. We're both definitely growing accustomed to this BDSM business, and it's becoming just another facet of our lives. The past few days have been slightly awkward. I haven't been planning scenarios, but instead we've been playing spontaneously, depending on whether both of us really wanted to. The problem with Catherine's work hours, and the associated stress, is that I never know what mood she'll be in when she arrives home. Yesterday, for instance, she was knackered when she got in; she'd left the house at 7 a.m. and arrived back home at 9.45 p.m. We decided that a bath and an early night to bed would do her a world of good. But, after her bath, Cat came into the bedroom where I was reading, and started blow-drying her hair. She had a towel wrapped around her, which gradually came undone and eventually slid off. The "bath and an early night" idea rapidly turned into a "spank and blow job" idea instead.

On the topic of spanking, I finally seem to be getting a bit better at it. I administered ten gentle slaps with my hand on each of Cat's arse cheeks to start, and then ten more, this time slightly harder. That was followed by twenty smacks on each cheek with the round paddle. I concluded the spanking session with ten gentle (if they can be called that) swings of the crop, followed by a second, harder set of ten. She seemed to enjoy that, a lot. But she wasn't completely wet yet, so I paddled her pussy ten times (softly) with the back of a large, flat brush. After that she was dripping, and my fingers easily slid into her. At last, I seem to be learning how to do this.

19 June 2010

I met an old friend for drinks tonight. I used to work with Mike, before we were both retrenched. Mike is great; he's smart, good-looking, has a good physique, he's funny, and is incredibly confident. Exactly the sort of person I usually cannot abide, but Mike is different from the norm. Along with his other traits he's also self-deprecating and humble, which renders all of the other characteristics irrelevant. Mike is married to Victoria, who is equally smart, has a good physique, and is funny and confident. And she's fucking hot.

Mike and I met for a few beers and a curry, and to discuss old times and bitch about the awful company we used to work for. We ate and we drank and we laughed. And then the most remarkable thing happened: Mike told me he wanted to be dominated. A group of women arrived, and sat at a table beside us. So of course, being typical men, our conversation turned almost instantly to which of them would "get it". It's puerile and dumb, but it's what men do; they imagine that any women entering their vicinity will immediately notice them, become smitten, and wish to procreate. I have long since discovered this is pretty much never the case.

Anyway, once we were done rating the contenders, Mike started telling me about his desire to have some strong woman order him about. He had mentioned this notion to Victoria in the past, and her response was to order him to wash the dishes. Vicky is apparently not at all interested in BDSM; they had occasionally tried a few things, like mild bondage and blindfolding, but it never worked for her. Besides, Mike was the one who wanted to be tied up. I think he probably expected me to be surprised, possibly even offended, and my reaction – one of understanding and support – seemed to really floor him. At this point in the conversation, I felt it was safe to confide that I had quite recently become a male counterpart of what he was looking for in a woman, and that my life had been altered, irrevocably, in the past few months. I was able to reveal quite a few facts to him about the BDSM community, based on all that I'd read. I assured him that he wasn't a freak or pervert, and that millions of people engage in kinky sex as an integral part of their lives. Unfortunately, I wasn't able to help him with his dilemma; he wanted to experience it, but was afraid to become involved, due to his commitment to Vicky. He wouldn't even consider the option of a visit to a professional dominatrix.

I drove home feeling very moved that Mike had revealed this side of himself to me, but also deeply saddened that he would possibly never know the thrill of being dominated. I know Catherine felt that emptiness, for so many years, before discovering D/s and opening up to me (well, Simon first, and then me), and her anxiety and misery was profound during that time. But, as much as I felt sorry for Mike and wished he could find a way to explore his submissive side, I was incredibly relieved that I'd been able to help Catherine realise her desires. There must be so many people out there who have no idea that a BDSM community even exists, and that they can find help and guidance about it without being made to feel like social outcasts.

20 June 2010

I've been rereading some parts of this diary (I guess because I'm still finding all of this a bit surreal, like I'm suddenly living someone else's life), and it occurred to me while doing so that there are likely a few other lost souls faced with a similar situation; men and women who are just as clueless as I was when I got sucked into this. I'm guessing it's not overly common to discover that your spouse/lover/ whatever has dark, secret desires. Who do you turn to and what can you do when your partner discovers there's a name for their inexplicable longing, and that an entire community exists who can help them learn more about their feelings?

So now I'm thinking that maybe I'll turn this little diary into a book instead. Maybe my experiences will help some poor clueless sod out there who feels like they just stumbled into a Dr Seuss world where nothing makes sense. I guess it would be a "how to" book. Specifically, *How to Beat on Someone You Love and Get Away with It*. Or at least it would be if you didn't follow the fundamental principle of BDSM, as I mentioned before: "Safe, Sane and Consensual". The practice of BDSM absolutely has to address the needs of *all* parties involved. It has to be about mutual fulfilment and equality, even though – on the surface or to the uninformed – it may not necessarily appear that way.

Throughout my adult life I've been an advocate of equality, whether it relates to race, sex, or religion. These constitute the fundamentals of a polite society, I guess; a place where most of us can live without the barbaric threat of someone else beating you to death with a club to steal the goat you've just hunted. Having been born and raised in Brazil, I was mostly indoctrinated into the practice of hatred based on nothing more than good old-fashioned slavery and a national penchant for violence. I found myself questioning these "values" for most of my life, until I finally left the country I love. Once we arrived in the United Kingdom, I found it incredibly liberating to not have that abiding sense of gloom and misery thrust into my face; people were completely comfortable interacting with those who happened to be born with a different skin colour, or believed in a different god.

As enlightened as I consider my views, since I met Catherine, my ideas and preconceptions relating to pretty much every aspect of my little world have needed updating. Cat is somewhat liberal in her attitude to life and to others. I thought I was equally open-minded. Yet Cat showed me that there is more to life than what happens inside my small globe of complacency. I'm accustomed to her challenging my way of seeing things. This time, though, she blew that world apart. And I thank her for that. I think.

22 June 2010

Cat and I have friends called Jenny and Bruce. Well, they're more like acquaintances. They're not close friends, just people we've known since Cat was pregnant with Robert. Catherine suspects that Jenny is almost certainly a dominatrix. Cat sees Jenny quite often, so I guess she's more able to form an opinion. I'd happily give Jenny a spanking, but that's another matter. From how well I know Bruce, I guess he fits into the sub role; he's pretty laid back, very quiet, but successful in his managerial position at work. Anyway, I was daydreaming earlier, and imagined inviting them over one night. I wouldn't tell Catherine about it, but while she was blindfolded on the bed with some music playing near her, I'd let them into the house and lead them into the bedroom. Then I'd tell Catherine to reach over and fondle my cock at the side of the bed. I'd make her suck it. And while she was doing that, I'd have Bruce stand silently beside me. After a few minutes, Bruce would tell Catherine how good her touch felt. No doubt she'd scream, and struggle to whip that blindfold off quicker than greased shit from a buttered plate. Then we'd all have a laugh and a few reassurances would follow about how everyone was really enjoying being so open about it all, and then the foursome could begin in earnest. Catherine did say she wanted spontaneity; that she wanted to be surprised on occasion. I reckon that would do it, although I suspect something so dramatic would probably undo Catherine's need for excitement, and could potentially end our marriage there and then. Or maybe she'd enjoy it and want to do even more outrageous shit next time. It could all turn out very messy, and quite possibly not in a good way. Especially if Jenny and Bruce are actually just vanilla.

23 June 2010

Catherine is going away for a week to a national educational conference near Manchester. A small part of me is wondering if Simon will be meeting her there, but that's a stupid and unproductive thought. And, so what if he is? Will I know about it either way? No. So shut up and move along.

I thought that, while Cat was away, the mouse could play. See what I did there? I'm a literary genius. OK, maybe not. Back to the point: I have a week to think up some ideas, to browse the internet and find new ways to amuse and excite my not-so-good lady wife.

25 June 2010

Cat texted me to say she'd arrived and was unpacking at her accommodation, a hotel near the venue. I replied, telling her to remove her panties once she'd unpacked, and then head down to the bar for a drink. After her drink was finished, she was to ask for a glass of ice and return to her room. Once back there I wanted her to strip and rub the ice over her naked body and, after five minutes of doing so, touch herself to warm up. She would be allowed to come. She messaged me back saying, *Yes, Sir*.

Later she texted and thanked me for allowing her to do that. I was pleased but, at the same time, I felt uneasy. The whole episode was mild and not very inspired. It had been spontaneous, yet it seemed dull. I felt frustrated and foolish, like the beginner that I am.

26 June 2010

I sent a text to Catherine this morning with our usual vanilla banter; saying hello, hoping her day goes well, that sort of thing. I told her right at the end that I wouldn't be sending her any further instructions while she was away, but that I would save up a few things for after she gets back home. She replied that was probably for the best, since she needed to focus on the conference. I can't help feeling that she was relieved by my suggestion.

1 July 2010

I had wanted to create a scenario that would blow us both out of the water. I read up on various ideas, jotted down a few I thought sounded exciting, and then lost interest. I'm so massively nervous about fucking this up. Cat has this thing inside her; this need, this animal that demands satisfaction. I thought I was capable of taming it, of controlling her and her desires. But now I'm doubting my ability to do so. I thought that some remote play while she was away would be exciting, but instead, because of the apathy with which I approached that, it feels like I've broken something. I have a sense that I've rushed into this D/s business blindly, in a panicked frenzy of fumbling ineptitude, grabbing with fragile fingers at a subject that is so much bigger than I am. I've never been hugely confident, and right now I'm feeling battered by a force I can do nothing to counter. Maybe I just need to chill out a bit, to read more, and make notes of things that I think will work for me as opposed to what will work for Catherine. But what will work for me? I have no idea. I've seen some pictures of people hanging from ropes; suspension bondage, I think it's called. I also read about something similar called Shibari, but I have no idea what the difference is. It looks more ornamental, which appeals to the artist in me. But the realist in me is wondering what the point of it is; all that work for what? To take a pretty photo when you're done? How is that stimulating, or in any way erotic for the sub? I just don't get it. I don't have that spark inside me that makes this feel natural; the magic ingredient that makes it all so exciting. In a way, I envy Cat for what she has, but at the same time I'm incredibly grateful I don't have to live with that need. And, because I don't get it, because I cannot grasp the fundamental basis of the BDSM dynamic, I seriously doubt that I can ever make this work properly, for either of us.

2 July 2010

Catherine arrived home just after midday. She went straight to bed and slept for four hours. Whether she's tired or not later, I figure tonight might be a good night to get back into the swing of things. I need to do it, if not for Catherine then for me, and for the sake of our marriage. Bad Dom, it's a two-way thing; both parties need to be fulfilled. You know what? Fuck that. I didn't write the rules. I don't need some pretentious pricks telling me how to enjoy some kink in my sex life, no matter how long they've been doing it. Yes, I'll go looking for hints and tips when it suits me to do so, but the whole "do it like this or it's not real" brigade can go fuck themselves.

3 July 2010

We played last night and, despite my anxiety, it was brilliant. Cat told me so this morning, and she seemed sincere about it.

It was a very simple play session: I made her strip and stand naked in front of me, hands clasped behind her back, and staring at the floor. She stood like that for half an hour, not making a sound. Then I grabbed her hair and forced her to her knees, making her suck my cock. I didn't come but, instead, yanked her head up and stared into her eyes, telling her she'd disappointed me by not being wet enough yet. I had no idea how wet she was, but this is all just role-playing, right? I sat on the edge of the bed and told her to crawl over to me, and drape herself over my knee. Then I spanked her with my open hands, thirty strokes on each arse cheek, alternating on every stroke. When her bum was glowing red I told her to lean on the bed, and I used the crop on her; ten strokes. After that I told her to lie on the bed and finger herself while I stood and watched. I ordered her not to make a sound, and every time she did, I used the crop on her upper thighs. When it looked like she was nearing orgasm I told her to stop, which she very reluctantly did. After that I bundled her up under the duvet and held her, telling her I'd wake her in the night and fuck her hard, at which time she would be allowed to come. She thanked me, and fell asleep quickly.

I lay there thinking about the session, considering what I'd done. It had all been spontaneous. I truly do not have a clue what I'm doing, but the whole scenario had just felt so right. I woke Cat an hour and a half later by entering her after I had smeared my cock with lube. She initially jerked awake and I held her down, taking immense pleasure from feeling her slowly wake up and relax under me, and start to enjoy what was happening. I came quickly, then turned her over and started touching her, rubbing my fingers over her pussy, then forcing them inside her. I used the fingers on my left hand to continue rubbing her clit, while the fingers on my right hand moved around inside her. I did this until she came. And when she did, it was massive.

6 July 2010

Catherine sent her best friend an email; a lengthy tome explaining all that had gone on, from her earliest thoughts that she was somehow different and later reading up about these strange desires, to discovering there is an entire community out there with hundreds of thousands of practitioners. She ended by explaining how she and I were tackling it together.

Lily and Cat have been friends since high school. They were both fiercely opposed to the educational, political, and social systems that constituted Brazilian society in the early 1990s. They both rebelled. They were staunch feminists, and were involved in any student protests involving race or gender politics. Lily hated school, and avoided attending whenever remotely possible, yet she achieved some of the highest grades in the history of the institution. She went on to become a professor of sociology. So she is pretty impressively bright, enlightened, and well informed. She is also homosexual and extremely visceral in her feminist standing. Nonetheless, Catherine wanted Lily to know what we were going through. She was therefore devastated by Lily's reaction, which was, to say the very least, explosive.

Lily was appalled by Cat's revelation. She was shocked and outraged. She attacked Catherine with a feminist rant that did not hold back in the slightest, and which ultimately threatened a friendship that had, for decades, been anchored in rock. I was touched by Lily's reaction, which radiated concern for both me and the boys. Lily was worried about what Cat's "condition" was ultimately going to do to our marriage. Was I really OK with it? Was I effectively being bullied into taking on the Dom role, in order to keep our marriage solid? Once Cat had recovered from the shock of the initial reply, she told Lily that we were all fine and were working our way through it as best we could. Catherine had tried to explain to Lily exactly how it felt to have finally discovered a name for what had been living inside her all her life, yet even with her knack for eloquence, she failed to convey the message as she had intended. As I've said before, submissiveness is not something that can easily be explained; I've read accounts by many subs trying to describe their feelings and why they need to be dominated and, to me, they all failed to provide a satisfactory explanation. Seeing Catherine's situation from a purely vanilla standpoint, I completely get why someone who is not into kink could so easily be freaked out by this lifestyle. But while Lily's response had completely blown Cat away, I can't say that I was too surprised, at all.

7 July 2010

I was lying in bed last night, having just written that last entry, and I got to thinking about the wider aspects of BDSM and its place in the "normal" world we all grew up in, with its values and moral righteousness and various other confining social structures. I'd heard about SM long before I even knew what sex was about. My family always joked about "whips and chains" but, since I was the youngest by a fair margin, I never had any idea what they were talking about. In the years since I was a child I've learned plenty of new things. I've seen videos on the internet when they first began streaming in Brazil in the mid-1990s. I've discovered that many humans are, in truth, just a bunch of bored degenerates. But for all that I've read and seen I still can't get my head around the fact that my wife is one of these kinky people. And now, so am I. Jesus wept.

As a teenager, once I'd discovered what the family was talking about with regard to whips and chains (not mentioned frequently, but perhaps just a bit too often to be entirely kosher), I considered people who were into SM to be freaks and weirdoes. Yet in my clubbing days, when I was surrounded by punks, Goths, and various others to whom society would instantly apply these labels, I never for a second viewed any of my fellow clubbers in any kind of negative way. In hindsight, many of those people who I associated with then were probably heavily into BDSM. I was oblivious to it. To me they were just people, out for a night of dancing, drinking, and socialising. Much like millions of others around the world, albeit with a penchant for alternative music. But for all the BDSM going on around me (I'm pretty certain of it, especially looking back on some of the conversations I had at the time, yet had no context for), these people never "infected" me. Just as gay people have never infected me. Oh and, surprisingly, nor have black people infected me. Nor any of the various other "negative" stereotypes that society has, over the millennia, branded evil or depraved. The uninformed, the blatantly ignorant, and the very worst of what we as a species have become, seemingly cannot help but blindly attack anything they do not and will not attempt to understand. I feel sorry for these bigots who are filled with a hatred fuelled by a lifetime of indoctrination. So many of them are convinced that their biased views are the absolute truth, due to being fed lies by small-minded friends or family members who convince them that their lofty ideals are earning them a ticket to a better place. Sadly, religion plays a massive role in this, as it always has in most things throughout history. But let's not go there. It's just not worth it.

I will readily raise my hand and admit that I once suffered from that same biased, blinkered view of what BDSM was all about, especially when Catherine first mentioned it to me (not all that long ago, but bloody hell, what a little bit of knowledge and some fun can do for you, eh?). My mind conjured up various inaccurate images gleaned from the very worst places: nasty internet sites, sleazy porn magazines, and cheap tabloid tat written by the husbands of housewives who knew someone who knew someone who did something involving whips. Now, of course, I'm better informed. But getting here took a hell of a lot of work and effort, and involved the incredibly difficult process of stretching my already wide open mind. God, what a sad and shitty little world we live in when people have the power to persecute others based on nothing more than rumours and speculation.

**Part Four
Dear Disaster**

22 July 2010

The inner strength required to maintain this is astounding. As a sub it's probably much easier, just doing as you're instructed, receiving what's given, and giving what's asked for. But, as a Dom, there are aspects to this that threaten to destroy mere mortals. Aside from the planning, the preparation, the hours of thought put into each scene, there are emotional barriers to confront. Getting my mind around the fact that I'm inflicting pain upon the person I love most in the world is an insanely tough thing to overcome. This woman, who I trust and respect for her fierce independence, for her intelligence, for her moral fortitude, is reduced (at my command) to a kneeling slave who will comply with my slightest request. Detaching one's mind from this lifestyle in order to continue with our everyday lives is just insane. Yet, in order to keep up appearances, we both need to go about the daily rigours as if nothing has changed. The responsibilities of looking after children (or, for Catherine, of having to concentrate on working a full day educating the masses), of doing menial tasks like going to the shops; these are all vital in maintaining equilibrium. It's quite difficult (although bizarrely, at the same time, somehow rewarding) seeing the same mums on the school run every day, all the while knowing Cat and I are secretly doing something that very few of the people we interact with in our daily pursuits even have a clue about.

24 July 2010

I spent all day yesterday stressing about our situation. I feel somewhat ambiguous about why I undertook this in the first place. I was desperate to rescue my marriage. Beyond that, not a hell of a lot of thought went into it, initially. I just hoped it would all work out.

Cat and I had a lovely evening, though. We shared a bottle of wine, ate a nice bolognaise that I'd cooked (the one thing I actually get right), and talked. It was so nice to just feel like an ordinary couple for a while. We decided to head straight upstairs for an early night – no TV, no work, no online gaming. We both showered and then just lay on the bed in our underwear, wishing it was cooler. Summer is finally here, after months of continual rain and cold; I'm not complaining, just setting the scene. Catherine and I shared an hour or so of absolute bliss, just softly touching and slithering over one another, ending with some gentle sex in the standard missionary position. We both came, and then snuggled into each other's arms. It dawned on us both that, actually, vanilla sex is probably what's been missing all this time. It was beautiful.

The D/s stuff is a completely different dynamic, which we both recognise. It's intense, hard, and requires a hell of a lot of mental and physical fortitude. I feel so much better today. Relieved, almost. Sex isn't the problem; too much D/s and not enough real life is the problem. I've been putting way too much into the BDSM side of our relationship, while trying to cope with kids and housework all day long. There isn't space for anything else. What I need to do is relax, stop trying too hard on the kink front, and just enjoy my life. My wife and children are my absolute first priority, but I guess it's easy to start neglecting your own self in that equation. I need to take care of me, first, and the rest will follow naturally. And if that requires "vanilla breaks" now and again, who am I to complain?

26 July 2010

Catherine and I had a long talk last night. For a few weeks I've had the feeling, each time we played, that something was missing. I've suspected for a while what it was: the cerebral aspect.

This is the part of the dynamic which is strongest for Catherine, but which I completely fail to address properly. The reason for that is pretty obvious: I just don't get it. I simply can't understand Catherine's needs, or which mental processes turn her on. After discussing this, at length, we decided my fumbling attempts are never going to work. We will both need to compromise. Catherine won't get the full scope of BDSM input from me, but I can no longer feel sick with worry that I'm not providing her with what she needs. I'll just do my best, using whatever methods work for us both, and which I'm capable of delivering. I'm not a natural Dominant, and so I shouldn't try to think like one. Of course I'll keep trying things, as and when they occur to me, but attempting to connect with "BDSM Catherine" on an equal footing is impossible, and therefore pointless. This realisation saddens me a great deal. I guess stepping into the Dom role saved a huge amount of misery and a potential marital break-up, so we should be grateful for that. Even so, I want to please my baby but I can't. And that's very difficult to reconcile.

28 July 2010

Just when I thought it was safe to go back into the bedroom ... Yet another messy, hormonal explosion. Catherine texted me to say that her studying for the master's degree wasn't going very well, and that she was heading into London to visit Carl.

I first met Carl in Brazil many years ago – before I knew Cat – when he and I worked together, and we became good friends. He later introduced me to an acquaintance of his; called Catherine ... and the rest is history. Carl moved to the UK a few years ago and now lives in London. He remains a mutual friend, and we both love him as dearly as if he were family.

I understand that Catherine needed to speak to someone about the stress in her life, and I also understand why it needed to be Carl. Even so, it was difficult to read the text she sent me. I had thought we were pretty much on track; that things were working really well between us. But – as ever – it seems they weren't. Two things in particular were not quite working.

Firstly, the master's degree. The fucking master's degree. God and baby Jesus, I wonder why Catherine ever thought that was a good idea. I wish I'd had the insight to tell her it wasn't. She would have done it anyway because she's Catherine, but I could have sat back now with my feet up, smug in the knowledge that I'd seen this coming. We'd still be having a shitty period right now, with no free time together, with every conceivable minute decimated by this blight called "work" that is necessary for her to progress on this path in life, and which everyone deems to be the driving force essential to keep our planet spinning.

And the second factor: D/s. Like I said, I thought we had that in check. I thought we'd conquered the demon that's been living inside Catherine for so long. I thought I was a promising Dominant, stumbling but succeeding in answering most of Catherine's needs. The physical ones, at least. Turns out I'm not. Honestly, though, I shouldn't be surprised. Like I said before, I wasn't convinced of it in my own head, so there was no way I was going to be doing anything useful for Catherine, who has thrice my brainpower. She obviously realised this a while ago, but hasn't wanted to hurt my feelings.

So, should I admit defeat now, instead of wasting more time agonising about what I'm doing wrong?

After Cat finally got home from London, once the boys were in bed, we talked. Same shit as before: she needs proper D/s input, and I can't provide it. She needs to get her kicks from somewhere, probably making contact with some unknown entity in the D/s community (or, potentially, even Simon again), but she also wants us to stay together. I struggled with hurting her physically because I cared too much, yet now I'm expected to stand by in the knowledge that someone *else* would be harming her? Previously, I had complete control over how much pain was inflicted, how much "peril" she was in. Now I'll have no idea what she's doing, or with whom. And if she takes it a step further, regularly meeting up with someone to play physically – what then? I've already told her I'm not interested in being her contact point for that, as someone to call if she's tied to a bed and her Dom has a coronary. She can ask Carl to be that contact. The poor sod. But, as a neutral party, he'll be the perfect go-between. Of course, what I would *like* is to know exactly what Catherine is doing at all times. I want to know who she's speaking to, who she's meeting, who she's playing with. But I respect her and I trust her. Sort of. I guess she wouldn't have told me anything in the first place if she was happy to mess around behind my back. I'll just have to believe that she's being careful and knows what she's doing.

Fuck a duck. What a shitty state of affairs. I feel an overwhelming desire to take care of my wife, to protect her. I can't do those things in this situation, and that sucks. I felt as if I was losing Catherine before, and then I felt as if I'd found her again, that our marriage was stronger than ever and, also, a lot more exciting. And now it's all in danger of turning to crap, again. I'm not sure how much more of this emotional bullshit I can take.

1 August 2010

I'm tired; tired of feeling so ridiculously out of my depth, tired of being removed from my comfort zone, and tired of all the turmoil in my life. Catherine has told me she's read about marriages that have undergone this same process. Some of them succeed but many more fail. I can understand the latter happening. I feel so lost, so helpless. Aside from a few shitty years of military service (which almost saw my exit from this mortal coil ... but that's all in a separate diary, none of which I feel able to reread or relate anytime soon), I've always been in control of my life. I pride myself on the fact that nobody dictates what happens in my head, and that my space, my mind, is my own. Yet, now, I'm faced with an impossible situation. I love this woman with all my heart, and would give my life in exchange for hers, but I'm having to choose between sharing her and losing her. Who could possibly decide on something so fundamentally important to their future, and to the future of their family? It's a fucking awful dilemma, to put it mildly. I have nowhere to turn on this. Catherine has Carl to talk to. He knows the story, and he knows us both very well. He's a great listener, which helps Catherine, at least. But who have I got to speak to; to offload on when things get rough? Nobody, that's who. Mike is a possibility, but he's having his own marital issues, and needs to address his own confused, kinky feelings. So, can I do this alone? Am I strong enough? If I think my family is worth it (I do, of course I do, and fuck Cat for putting us all in this situation due to her own selfish needs), then I'll just have to make sure that I am.

12 August 2010

Catherine and I are doing vanilla, exclusively, right now. Cat told me earlier, 'It feels like coming home.' She's probably getting her D/s fix elsewhere; maybe speaking to people online, making arrangements or playing or whatever. Do I care? Of course I do. Do I want to know what she's up to? Hell, yes. But I can't pry. I owe it to both of us not to. The last time I asked too many questions, my life fell apart. So what do I do? I'm a curious creature. I can't stand not knowing. But I need to not know, for both our sakes. Maybe she hasn't started playing yet, but she will. I know it. It's only a matter of time. Will she go crawling back to Simon (on all fours, wearing a collar. Ha ha. Christ!)? Or will she find someone new? I hate not knowing. I need to know. But I need to not know even more.

I should be content that our sex lives have resorted to normal again. Well, with a tiny bit of naughtiness thrown in occasionally; nipple tweaks, bites, scratches, and so on. Not strictly D/s, but just some extra spice that we didn't have in the past. I've told Catherine I'm happy to have a kinky play session again, some time, but she was slightly reticent about it. She still thinks I was distressed about the spanking aspect, about the pain I had to inflict. At first, I was, but I got used to it; it's what Catherine wanted, so that's what I gave her. Albeit cautiously and without any real authority, which is why it failed for her. But it wasn't all about the pain, for me; it was more about the pressure to perform. I've probably mentioned that a few times in some of the entries I wrote while we were playing and experimenting. Somewhere deep inside, a little voice is screaming at me to man up; to become a sadistic bastard and start enjoying beating people up. But I don't want to do that. Certainly not to someone I love.

Let's see how this "vanilla at home with Cat playing on the side" idea works. I hope to God we've finally sorted it out.

17 August 2010

I had a dream, a couple of nights ago, in which Catherine was blindfolded and tied to a chair (fully dressed). Some guy in a smart suit and full-face leather mask was standing over her, whispering, 'You can cry all you want, but nobody can hear you.' I was observing a scene whereby Catherine was effectively being held captive – I couldn't tell if it was a play scene or not – and it freaked me out, immensely. I told her about it the next day and she just shrugged. It seems all the angst and chaos going on inside me is irrelevant to her. All she seems to think about is herself, and that's starting to piss me off.

19 August 2010

I've been afraid to say anything to anyone about all of this, but it's been eating me up inside. I needed to get it off my chest. So I took the plunge and told my best mate, Harry, what was happening between Cat and I.

Vanilla Harry, terribly straight, was subjected to all the gory details, from the very start. When I'd finished he said to me, quite simply, 'I always wanted a Porsche, but I know I'll never have one so I just have to move on.' There's a reason he's my best friend; Harry is utterly, incredibly, fucking cool. Non-judgmental, level-headed… just cool. We drank beer, we discussed stuff a bit more, and we laughed. It was exactly what I needed, and I wondered why I'd felt unable to speak to him before now. I guess Lily's apoplectic reaction to Cat's confession had something to do with that, and I'd been scared that I could also end up losing a friend.

When we were saying goodbye, afterwards, in the parking lot, Harry hugged me and told me to be strong. His reaction – and knowing that I finally have someone I can talk to about this – is massively comforting.

Harry's comment about the Porsche made me think. I realised that throughout all of this bullshit, I have never once asked Catherine whether she realises this is, potentially, something she'll have to live without, if we're planning to stay together. I've never requested that she just consider it as a "nice to have" element in her life. If I understood the BDSM dynamic a bit more, if D/s was part of who I am, as it seems to be with Catherine, then – well, obviously – things could be so different. But I don't understand it. I don't like it, or the idea of it, and I refuse to have my life dictated by it.

4 September 2010

What kind of an idiot helps someone else achieve all of their life's ambitions, while watching their own dreams die?

I'm so lost. What the hell can I do? I'm supporting Catherine as she builds her ideal life, yet I'm miserable, probably to the point of needing medical intervention. Why am I doing this? Yes, I was raised to help others, to speak the truth at all times and never betray trust, but is it worth it? Is it fucking worth it?

I was also raised to think for myself, yet here I am being buried under a mountain of bullshit that has not been, even in the slightest, of my own making.

5 September 2010: a letter, unsent

Cat,

You told me a while back that your newfound kinkiness elevated your sexual needs. Seems that's fallen by the wayside, somewhat. Your play with Simon seems to address those requirements. I almost feel like you're doing me a favour every time we have sex.

For so many years I felt like I'd won first prize: a beautiful, funny, intelligent, amazing person, the girl of my dreams, had chosen me! But now I feel like I'm coming second, like I've been shoved aside for someone more exciting. And that feeling sucks.

You have your friends for support, you have your colleagues to discuss work with, and you have someone else in your life, now, as a companion and to fulfil your every fantasy and desire, and to address that most basic human need. But you and I have reached a point where I have nothing left to offer you. And you don't need me any more.

So if it feels like I'm distancing myself from you, it's because I am. I'll be your housekeeper and I'll be your childminder. And in return I expect to be housed and fed, and will need financial assistance to cover the monthly debits coming off my bank account. I expect and I offer nothing more.

7 September 2010

What if I were to have an affair? Or, if not an affair as such, then a D/s relationship with another person. How would Cat feel about that? I asked her about it earlier, and she would apparently be absolutely fine with that.

Many years ago, long before I met Catherine, I remember wondering why people couldn't just enjoy polygamous relationships. It sounded like a great idea to me. Why do we need to be faithful to one partner all our lives? Monogamy's not natural; it's a rite that has been foisted upon us through centuries of tradition, mostly enforced by brutish misogynists and adulterers hiding behind masks of piety, who truly believe they are protecting us from ourselves. And I always thought I'd be absolutely fine with polygamous, open relationships; if my wife would allow me to dabble with others, then I'd be OK with her having extramarital affairs too. So long as everyone was happy and having fun, then what harm, right? How wrong I was. When it actually came to Catherine doing anything with someone else – hell, not even doing anything, just thinking about doing it – I fell to pieces. So much for being a liberal thinker.

10 September 2010

OK, things aren't going very well here. Cat and I

seem to be in a sort of dead space, ignoring the fact that we had this dynamic, crazy ride just a short while ago, which has now descended into an awkward period of non-disclosure. I know that Cat won't give up on this BDSM stuff; it's inside her, and she has now physically experienced it, first-hand. Thanks to me, and you're very welcome indeed. Feels like I've cut my own fucking throat. What a douche. How did I ever think I had what it takes to be a Dominant? It's not natural to me. Yes, I made it work through sheer bloody-mindedness and determination, but it was difficult. None of the ideas came naturally to me, and I never once felt excited at the prospect of hurting someone else. Cat's physical and emotional responses to what I was doing turned me on, but the acts themselves didn't quite get there. So I'm not a natural or true Dom. That doesn't bother me. What *does* bother me is the fact that I failed, and Cat will now be looking elsewhere for her kicks. I need to be OK with that, because I've told her that I will try to be. But I'm not, and I never will be; that's a given. I'm stuck in an extremely shitty place. I love Catherine, as much as I ever have, but there's a growing resentment in me that I just can't shake. Yet for the sake of the children, I need to do just that. I almost said "for the sake of my marriage", but deep down I know that's over. There's nothing else I can do except grin and bear it. I'll do my best, but the knowledge that another man is having his dick sucked by my wife will never feel acceptable. I'm still far too vanilla for that to be right in my head. I have absolutely no idea what to do.

**Part Five
Dear Head Trip**

Author's note

During this frustrating and highly emotional period, I had no idea what my future would hold. I was rereading parts of this diary from when Cat had first told me about her submissiveness. I think I knew, even then, that my marriage was going downhill. At the point of writing my previous entry, I was fed up with the situation. I didn't feel like writing a diary any more, so I attempted to finish it off with an imagined scenario of what could possibly happen in the days and weeks to come. I had never really wanted to remain in the United Kingdom but, equally, I held no strong desire to return to Brazil. However, my family and good friends were all there, the weather was a lot better, and the idea of being back in my home country, albeit somewhere new and unexplored, gave me a sense of comfort and held the promise of freedom. I had long heard that São Paulo is an amazingly vibrant city, with the additional bonus of being a bit more liberal than other parts of the country. I'd been thinking for a while that it could be the ideal place to make a fresh start, if everything turned to shit.

This chapter is what I wrote as an imagined "ending" to my saga. Nothing in this section of my diary actually happened. However, the idea of it was very appealing at the time, and remained so afterwards. And as you will see, the irony of my make-believe scenario becomes poignantly relevant further down the line.

Fictional Entry Number One

We're splitting up.

I've had it. I'm nowhere near as strong or resilient as I thought I was, which sucks. I sent Catherine a text earlier that went like this:

You and I share something profound, and deep, and intimate. I can safely say that I will never love another the way I love you. I will always know this.

However, I can't be a party to events that I'm uncomfortable with, or which compromise my feelings for you. Similarly, I won't stay here simply to act as a househusband, a carer and cleaner, while you're out cavorting with God-knows who.

Maybe I'll have other relationships, and maybe I'll even enjoy some of them.

In light of everything that's happened, and everything I suspect will happen, I feel the time has come for me to make a break. I've tried to fix us, and I've failed. I've put my own needs and happiness aside for too long in order to save our marriage, yet nothing I've done has made any difference.

I can't do this any more. So I'm leaving. I'm going far away from here, to live an uncomplicated, sane life.

Good luck finding what you're looking for. Please be careful.

Fictional Entry Number Two

Well, that's been the shittiest time of my life, which is saying something.

Everything that came before pales in comparison to the trauma of what's been happening over the past few weeks. I've had to face Catherine's grief, and then anger, regarding my departure. But that was nothing balanced against the fact that I'm leaving my children. I've had to carry on with everyday life, packing school lunches, bathing the boys, and putting them to bed, in the full knowledge that I'm going to have to say goodbye to my two little people so very soon. Those precious, wonderful children have no idea what's going on; that there are fierce storms occurring around them which will soon blow their house down. They have not had a single thing to do with the massive change that is about to destroy their lives as they know them, and that's the worst part. I'm doing this because I'm selfish. This is my issue; my need to escape a situation that I can't handle. Christ. What kind of father willingly abandons his own children?

Enough writing. I need to pack.

Fictional Entry Number Three

So. Dear diary. Here we are again. Just the two of us.

Well, I'm in Brazil. I made it. I thought this move would be easy. How wrong can any one person be?

Leaving the UK was insane. I feel broken just thinking about it, remembering traumatised and emotion-filled fragments of those last few hours.

Would it have been easier if Catherine and I didn't love each other? If we'd argued, and fought, and ended up hating one another? Probably not.

I cannot and will not ever forget the look on Robert's little face as I told him I was leaving. I tried so hard to keep it together, but of course I failed. My wonderful little boy, six years old, confused as only an innocent child can be, as I hugged him so tight that it must have hurt. He expects me to return; to come back home after my holiday. How could I possibly explain to that sweet kid that I was going away for a very long time, possibly forever, and that it had nothing to do with him? What sense could he make from me telling him that Mummy and I still love each other but aren't going to be together any more? I felt my heart breaking as I stared into his huge eyes. James was oblivious; too busy running around causing chaos, yelling, and getting in the way of people who were trying to push past us in the airport terminal. Bless the little bastard, I'll miss him, too.

Whoever wants to be in that situation? I told Catherine a few times, in that last week, that I was leaving in order to avoid causing resentment later on. Yet, as I sit here, I resent her for not stopping me from leaving. She gave in to her desires, decided that her sexual fulfilment was more important than her family. And yes, of course, I resent that. Who in their right mind would not? I realise that she is facing demons beyond my understanding, but how, as an intelligent, rational adult, could she not see what her issues were doing to the rest of us? Fuck her for that. I love her so much that it hurts. But do I like her? No.

I haven't liked her for a very long time.

Fictional Entry Number Four

I'm moving out of Jack's house next week. Jack is my brother; not sure I've mentioned that before now. Jack and his wife, Sarah, took me in to live with them after my separation. The last of their kids left home a few years ago, so they had space. I told them that Cat and I were having a difficult patch due to her work, and that looking after the boys on my own had become too stressful. Oh, look, a sword to fall on. But you know what? I don't care what people think of me. I'm doing this to save my sanity, and to give my children a secure future. Blah blah, they need their dad, blah blah. Bullshit. They don't need someone who is living on a razor's edge, wondering if each day will be the one that finally ends with an overdose. So I've been shacking up here, in a very comfortable house on the outskirts of Rio.

After a few months of sitting on my arse and feeling like shit, I finally managed to land a job in São Paulo. That's not especially close to most of my family, but it's a fresh start.

I can't reveal the truth to anyone about what happened, yet they still pry and sympathise with my somewhat inaccurate reasons for why I left. I've tried to keep Catherine's name clean, when all I want to do is tell them what a deviant she is, and how she twisted our lives inside out. But that would be unfair to her. She's done nothing wrong. Not really. I still feel slightly sad for her every time I think about it; about what an impossible situation she found herself in. I wish I could have given in, and let her play with another person, without feeling like she was somehow betraying me. But I know myself too well. Hell, I should do, after so many years of having to deal with the turmoil and anger in my own head. I just wouldn't have been able to handle it, and our relationship would have ended really, really badly.

So yeah, I'm off to São Paulo. Jack is lending me the money I need to set myself up until my salary starts coming through. I've found a flat to rent, and I have a week to sort my shit out. Fortunately, I'm not some wide-eyed college kid who doesn't have a clue about life. I know what I need. Materially, at least. For the flat, just the essentials: a fridge, a washing machine, a stove, cutlery, crockery, pots and pans, a kettle, and a toaster. And a bed. Probably a lamp, too, and an alarm clock. I'd love a massive TV with a gaming console, but that may have to wait. That should be me sorted, aside from curtains and a few bags of assorted groceries and various sundry items. All I need now is my wife and children, and it'd feel just like home.

Fictional Entry Number Five

Hello, diary. It's been too long. We really must do this more often.

I'm entrenched in my new digs. São Paulo is brilliant. I've been here about three months now. The apartment is great. I expected constant noise, being in the city centre, but it's actually pretty quiet. Thank the gods.

The new job is going well. I'm with a small

business, and everyone who works here has been pretty pleasant, so far. One woman is of particular interest; she's absolutely stunning. Her name is Gabriella. I'm sure she could be a successful model or something, but she just wants to write code for an IT company. I mean ... what? Not that I'm complaining. Very nice eye candy, even if she hasn't actually noticed that I exist. Same as it ever was, then. The guy she's engaged to is one of the founders of the business, some stiff-collared posh boy called Eduardo. He's a complete knob. Actually, in all fairness, I probably only think that because he gets to bang Gabriella, every night of his life. Anyway, everyone else is really friendly, and the work is interesting. So that's nice.

Fictional Entry Number Six

Life is good. We had a social thing at work last week. It was Friday afternoon, with free drinks being served on the office balcony overlooking the park. I was leaning against the railing and enjoying the view when Gabriella was suddenly next to me. Like, *right* next to me. She asked if I wanted to buy her a drink. I laughed and said she could ask the barman for a vodka and Coke, and to put it on my tab. She thought that was funny. My heart was beating like a train; I was being giggled at (in a good way, for once) by a stunning woman, who I had previously watched from afar, and who I'd thought wasn't even aware I was alive. Yet here she was, slightly tipsy but not drunk, and flirting with me. Her boyfriend was off with his fellow directors, playing golf, and would probably end up talking about racing cars and drinking whisky that costs more than my monthly rent. But I couldn't care less.

Half an hour later, Gabriella and I were locked in the financial director's office, rolling around on the carpet and thrusting ourselves at each other like animals. She was going at it with the enthusiasm of a pig at a trough, and at one point I raised my arm to smack her bare arse. I stopped myself just in time, but have since wondered what might have happened if I hadn't.

Fictional Entry Number Seven

Wow. Gabriella. Who would have thought it? An oik like me, unmoneyed, uncultured, and vastly uneducated, getting laid by the best-put-together genetic package I've come across (literally) in a very long while. I'm amazed. I haven't asked her why she wanted me, and I never will. Gift horses, and all that sort of thing. But, if she's bored with her preppy fiancé and I'm a temporary distraction, then so be it. Who am I to complain?

Yet ... something's missing. For all the freedom I'm feeling, for all the amazing sex I'm having with Gabriella, for all the motorbike rides I'm taking up and down the stunning coastline ... for all that, I still feel empty. I miss my boys, terribly. And every time I think of my beautiful Catherine's sad, brave smile as she waved goodbye, I crumble inside. How could I have left them like that? What kind of selfish, conceited tosser does that to his family? Catherine had a gap in her life, something fundamental within her that needed exploring and, instead of allowing her to embark on what should have been an exciting and wonderful quest to find out more about herself, I forced her to suppress it. I'm such a fucking idiot.

Fictional Entry Number Eight

I've spoken to Catherine a few times recently – more often than the usual weekly phone call to speak to her and the kids – and asked how things were. She said the boys were confused and missed their daddy. That broke my heart. She told me they were both doing well at school, but Robert has become far less bubbly. That wonderful kid used to be such a happy little soul and, of course, it's only since I left that this is happening. James was probably still too young to realise the significance of what was happening, or to miss me too much. Catherine is apparently working hard, and not spending much time at home. So that much has stayed the same, at least. The au pair is wonderful – we were really lucky to find her. Cat and I interviewed a few potentials before I left, and this one (Frances) immediately stood out. The kids love her, and she actually spends time playing with them, which I seldom did. So from that aspect it's working out pretty well.

Catherine says she's started playing again – online only – with some guy called Mark but, because she works so much, she hardly ever gets to do anything. And, when she does, she's often exhausted and doesn't get very much out of it. She hasn't met him yet, and doesn't envisage that happening anytime soon. Probably because their D/s relationship hasn't really had time to get off the ground. So all my fears about her messing around and being gang-banged seem pretty much unfounded.

I'm feeling pretty shitty about everything right now. I've ruined their lives. Can I live with that? Can I be OK in the knowledge that people I care for are worse off because I'm not with them? I need to get some sleep.

Fictional Entry Number Nine

I'm being eaten alive by guilt. I'm having a great life here, but my children are missing me and my wife sounds like she's on the verge of a breakdown. Cat hasn't said as much, but I can tell how tired she is, every time I speak to her. She sounds drained and miserable. She's an incredibly strong person, but I still worry about her. My initial lease on this apartment runs out at the end of next month. I've got a lot to think about before then.

Fictional Entry Number Ten

Gabriella wanted to know if we were going anywhere with our relationship. What relationship? We just fuck! I didn't say that, of course; I'm far too chicken-shit to deploy my usual in-your-face honesty right now. She's thinking about leaving Eduardo. So we got into an argument. I said I thought we'd just agreed to have uncomplicated, random sexual encounters as and when the opportunity arose and, if she was serious about leaving that arsehole, then she should just do it and not use me as a decider. She said she didn't know what to think; that I kept moping around and talking about my family and, if I was so unhappy, then I should leave and go back to them. She may have a point. While I was pondering that, she made some frustrated sound, threw her arms in the air, and stormed out of my flat. I'm thinking that maybe Gabriella isn't much of a trophy after all.

I need a beer. I'm thinking about heading to Snappy Sam's for a few pints. I know alcohol is never a solution but, right now, I don't really give a fuck.

Fictional Entry Number Eleven

Alcohol. Great stuff. Pff.

Strange how having a few drinks always seems so clever at the time. Well, lo and behold, it rarely is. It fixes nothing. I've been in a haze for a while now. The day after Gabriella and I argued, she decided I wasn't worth the effort. She told Eduardo that we'd been seeing each other, and the limp-dick retaliated by telling me that the company wouldn't be keeping me on, once my initial contract period was up in a few weeks. I told him exactly what I thought of him and his rich, spoiled upbringing (not that I know a thing at all about his upbringing, but I had a hangover at the time and it seemed like a good idea), and he threatened to sue me. What a complete prick. Nobody appreciates honesty any more.

So yeah, no more job, no more supermodel fuck-buddy. Strangely, though, it's cleared my mind. Well, after a few days of binge-drinking and feeling sorry for myself, that is. Getting dog-arsed drunk for a week and waking up in an alleyway – twice – has made me realise just how miserable I've been. Yes, the weather here is brilliant, yes, I'm free to come and go as I please, and yes, it's been exciting sleeping with someone new. But it hasn't felt right. None of it has. Not for a minute. I don't belong here. I have people elsewhere who need me. My worthless, selfish, grumpy self is wanted somewhere on this planet, and I've ignored that fact for far too long. Time to man up.

Fictional Entry Number Twelve

England, my England. I arrived back here four days ago. My beautiful family were there to greet me, and it was the greatest moment of my life. I cried like a baby, seeing them all again. I can't believe how my boys have grown in just a few short months. And Catherine seems happy to have me back (not that she was effusive about it in a public area, but she emitted a positive vibe in her own quiet, understated way).

So. I'm home.

Not much has changed. Frances (the au pair) had moved things around a bit, so the telly was where my PC had been. I'm writing this in the study now, transferring recent entries from my trusty (if somewhat battered) old notebook onto Catherine's laptop. The kids are at school, and Frances is sorting out a few bits of paperwork in preparation for her next job. I think she resents me for coming back (well, possibly for leaving in the first place, too), but she's young, and she has no idea what we've been through. Catherine is at work, having spent the past two days here with me. We spent Sunday – the day after I arrived – together as a family. It initially felt a bit foreign but, after a short while, everything started feeling natural again, like nothing had changed. Bizarre. I think Catherine is genuinely happy, and possibly relieved, to have me here. From my side, it feels like a massive weight has been lifted from my shoulders. I'm sleeping in the lounge, which is fine. I'll probably get the spare bed in the study once Frances has left. Or maybe, if things go really well, I'll be invited back into our bedroom …

Fictional Entry Number Thirteen

I spoke to Catherine about the D/s stuff. She said she hadn't spoken to or played with Mark for over a week, just wanting to focus instead on me returning and seeing how that worked out. I told her I don't care what she does with Mark – or anyone else for that matter – and I really meant it. Or maybe I'm just trying to convince myself of that. She needs to explore, to find herself (how clichéd does *that* sound!). She said, unsurprisingly, that she didn't want to think about that right now.

I need to start looking for a job. Having both kids at school means I have no excuse to stay at home during the day any more. We'll make a plan with Denise (a child-minder a few houses away, and an old friend) to drop off and fetch the boys, and we'll collect them after work. So life carries on, as if nothing ever happened.

But something did happen: I discovered that I'm not the selfish person I thought I was. I put the needs of my family above my own. I put other people first. And that's never happened. I felt guilt and remorse for leaving, and I fixed that. So I'm feeling pretty OK about my life right now. I hope that feeling lasts.

Fictional Entry Number Fourteen

Started looking for work today. Nothing to report so far. The market is dead.

Fictional Entry Number Fifteen

Just like that, I got a phone call from an agency wondering if I'd be interested in a job less than five miles away. I fitted their criteria perfectly. I attended an interview, got called back for a second interview a week later, and they offered me the post, starting at the beginning of next week. The salary is a drop from what I was getting at the previous UK company I worked for, but it's a start. Frankly, I don't care. I'm trying to rebuild my life, and gainful employment is a massive piece of that puzzle. Even if the job's shit and I hate everyone there, it's fine. Life is a pile of bricks – if you're not crushed by their weight and constant state of shift, you need to build something useful with them.

Fictional Entry Number Sixteen

Hello, diary.
    A year and a half on, I remembered you exist. Ha

ha! We were so close when things were shit and, just like that, everything picks up again and you're forgotten. Apologies, if I'm being fickle, but you *are* just a book.

I'm enjoying my job. Never thought I'd enjoy working again, to be honest. The work is constant, and it's challenging. I can drop Rob and Jamie at school in the mornings (both of them are at "big" school now), and pick them up from the child minder's place at 5.30, so we're not paying too much in care costs. The money issue has eased up, which means there's one less source of stress in our lives.

On the D/s front, things have become interesting. I play with Catherine, every now and again, but not properly; we occasionally just have kinky sex (tying wrists, blindfolds, pulling hair, and the occasional slap on the arse). She's into D/s mainly to address the psychological aspect, and this she gets with Mark, which is fine by me. My generous approach to her messing around with someone else is probably facilitated by the fact that I'm playing with another woman. Catherine knows about it, of course – we've been completely open and honest about everything since we got back together.

Fictional Entry Number Seventeen

I had to stop writing and go sort out the boys' dinner/bath/bed routine before I could elaborate on my new "friend" in that last entry. Here we go, then:

Her name is Faith. We met at our local village pub (of all places), when I randomly got together with my work colleague, Matt, for a drink, about three months ago. Matt and I car-share because he lives in the next village down. Faith is one of the mums I've seen on the school run in the past. She was always really attractive and worth a second glance, but seemed to avoid eye contact. I spotted her chatting to another mum at the pub when we walked in but, as ever, she seemed to ignore me. When I went to the bar to order a drink, she sidled up to me and started chatting; trivial stuff, mostly about the school – common ground, I guess. Then, out of the blue, she told me she'd split from her husband, and said she was pretty lonely aside from the company of a few other mums. Oh, and she also suggested I should bring the boys over for a play-date at some point. I'm not sure what she expected me to say, but I replied that that sounded like a good idea. She told me to give her a call the following week to arrange something, and gave me her number. I was intrigued.

I phoned Faith the following week, and she said she'd been waiting for my call. She invited me over that afternoon, and gave me her address. I took the kids to her place after school. I knew that it was all a bit farcical – my intuition is pretty rubbish, but I had a feeling that she was interested in a bit more than a cup of tea. We chatted a bit, and she was actually really good company; her husband's work had taken her around the world, and she had quite a few anecdotes to relate. I vaguely noticed the children all heading upstairs at some point, but what was of more interest was how she'd moved closer to me on the sofa. She was obviously flirting; her eyes were sparkling and, every time I said something even vaguely amusing, she'd laugh and touch my arm in that "oh, you're so funny" manner that some people have. She asked me what I do for fun, and I couldn't resist telling her that I liked tying people up and smacking their arses. She was speechless for a few seconds, just staring at me. I told her I was joking, and she looked dubious. When she said, 'So you don't really do that?' I asked her what she thought. She looked at me suspiciously. And then she cleared her throat and told me, completely straight-faced, that she'd always wanted to try that. I thought I'd have a heart attack. The kids came back downstairs then. James had hurt his arm and was wailing (well done on your timing, son; maybe next time don't jump off the fucking bed and onto the side table) and so I said we'd continue our conversation another time, and left. Faith looked genuinely disappointed.

We spent the next few days texting back and forth. Faith was intrigued by what I had to offer. I was modest in relating my experience, but she didn't care. The more we texted, the more she revealed how kinky she really was. I told her I would make a plan to come over again, soon, this time without the boys.

Later that week I mentioned to Catherine that I was going to start playing with someone else, and she surprised me by initially looking quite shocked. I think she quickly realised that this was a two-way street, though, and seemed almost relieved. Less guilt-ridden, at least. She said, 'Cool. Be careful.' And that was that.

I took a day of annual leave from work, and visited Faith at her house, the following week. Her husband had moved in with a younger woman a couple of months previously, but was repentant enough to leave his mansion to Faith and the kids. So we had a massive playpen, all to ourselves.

We started our day with a cup of tea and some idle gossip at the kitchen table. Then I related the basics of what we were about to do. I told Faith that whatever we did, it would not involve any actual sexual contact until she requested it. I said I'd be ordering her to do various things, and that she needed to comply up to the point where she no longer felt comfortable, at which time she needed to tell me a "safe word", indicating her desire to cease all activities. She decided on "teddy bear". I told her to lead me into the bedroom, which she did. She asked if she should get undressed, and I told her no. She seemed really surprised, even disappointed, and I laughed. Not very "professional Dom", but I couldn't help it. I apologised, and told her I was going to take it slowly and teach her, very gradually, what D/s was all about. Faith seemed to become more excited then, or maybe she was nervous; I'm not too good at reading women.

There are so many books out there regarding D/s: how to do it, what rules to follow, what to say, and so on. I've read a few, and the only useful thing that I gleaned from any of them was the fact that, whatever is done, it needs to be safe, sane, and consensual – the fundamentals of BDSM, and common sense for any normal human being. I explained to Faith that being tied up meant being completely under my control. I stated, emphatically, that she needed to understand this concept, and feel safe about it. She told me that she'd had her eye on me for years (I'd never noticed? God …) and she felt she could trust me.

I ordered Faith to blindfold herself with one of those little eye-mask thingies you get on a long-haul flight. It was the same blindfold I'd used with Catherine, which felt really weird and a bit awkward for me. While she did that, I brought in a sturdy wooden chair from the dining room. When I got to the bedroom she told me she didn't know what to do, and that she felt a bit silly. I assured her that I'd done this sort of thing before and all she needed to do was relax and enjoy it. But if she felt at all uncomfortable, she was to use her safe word. I made her repeat her safe word, and asked if she was ready. She nodded.

I positioned myself behind her, checked that the blindfold was on properly, and moved her hair out of the way, gently brushing it off her neck. Faith flinched slightly and moaned, probably inadvertently. I put both of my hands around her waist and asked if she was OK. She said yes, but was shaking slightly. Her body felt amazing, and I was briefly smacked upside the head by a pang of guilt before remembering that I had the go-ahead from Catherine. That knowledge didn't seem to make it any easier. But still. I'm human, and being here and doing this was driving me crazy with excitement and arousal. I made sure not to let Faith know how I felt; it's all theatre, which I guess is half the fun. I placed the palm of my hand in the small of her back and gently pushed her towards the chair, telling her to move forward. I stopped her, moved the chair into position, and then sat her down. Her legs were together, hands folded on her lap. I told her we were going to have a very gentle first session.

I lifted Faith's hands slightly, asked her if she was

ready (she said yes), and then bound her wrists with a cotton rope. I looped the rope under her breasts a few times, again, "accidentally" brushing them on occasion. By this stage I was as hard as a pole. After that, I tightened the rope before knotting it behind the chair. I was behind the chair, and I tilted her head back a little, holding it with both my hands. I put my mouth close to her ear and asked if the rope was too tight. The sound she made was almost a squeak, and it took all of my willpower to not burst out laughing. I think she said no. I held my grip for a while longer, breathing softly into her ear, then said, 'Good,' and let go.

I moved to stand in front of her, where I waited for a full two minutes. To her credit, Faith never budged, and didn't ask what was happening. I knelt in front of her, placing my hands on her knees. She jumped a bit. 'How will I do this?' I pondered, just loudly enough for her to hear. I stroked the outer sides of her thighs, held my fingers there for a while, and then moved them slowly over the top and towards her inner thighs, pausing halfway between her knees and crotch. She opened her legs very slightly, and I used that opportunity to spread them wider, gently but forcibly. Faith gasped, and I smiled in satisfaction.

I used a second rope to bind her ankles and then her knees to the chair legs. I told her to stay like that; to not move no matter what. I stood watching her for the following five minutes. I also took in a few details about my surroundings: the family photos, the immaculate dressing table, tidy shelves, and clean surfaces. Faith was either very house-proud, or she used a cleaning service. She was neat, which was good. And she was very attractive, with an amazing body. I considered my sagging face and expanding stomach, my receding hairline and deepening wrinkles, and I smiled. I've never been much of a ladies' man, but I seemed to be doing OK right about now.

I could never, in my wildest dreams, have imagined myself doing something like this with another woman after I'd met Cat. I moved to stand behind Faith's chair again. Theatre. I was playing my part, being a gentleman, when all I really wanted was to fuck her silly. Well, maybe not all of me wanted that; a small part was still seething with furious guilt. But it was a very tiny part, and a somewhat larger part was seething equally fiercely, not with guilt but with lust. Putting my face beside hers again, I tested the ropes around Faith's breasts, and asked her if they were too tight. She sighed, 'No.' After a while, I moved around, placed my right hand on her inner thigh, and edged slowly towards her pussy. Just before touching, I stopped and held my hand there. Faith was wearing jeans, so I couldn't tell how wet this was making her. I had a rough idea, though, based on how much she was squirming under my touch, and how heavily she was breathing. I stood, moving away from her. I asked if she was turned on. She replied simply, 'Yes.' I asked if she wanted to escalate things. She paused, and then asked what I meant. I reminded her that we'd decided there would be no sexual contact until she said so. I told her that none was required; that I could do things to excite her without either of us getting undressed. She said, 'I'd like you to touch me … everywhere.' And so I did.

Fictional Entry Number Eighteen

My relationship with Faith continued for four weeks before we discussed sexual contact again. We hadn't had sex during our first play scene, but I had used my hands and made her come more times than she could count (or so she told me afterwards). But I hadn't let her touch me at all; I hadn't even been undressed in her presence. I had used my fingers on and in her again during other sessions, as well as dildos and vibrators. Faith blurted out during one scene that she needed to be fucked. She seemed shocked as she said it (she was naked and tied to the bedposts at the time, and I was giving her a few gentle taps on the pussy with a plastic ruler). I stopped the session, untied her, and explained that the Dom/sub relationship sometimes involved oral sex given by the sub, or penetration (anal and/or vaginal) by the Dom. Faith seemed very willing to try any and all of those activities. I was surprised to find myself speaking so knowledgeably about the lifestyle; I'm a complete novice, for fuck's sake!

I'd spoken to Catherine about the possibility of me having sex with another woman. Catherine didn't seem happy about it, but said that she understood the Dominant/submissive relationship, and that this outcome would probably be inevitable. She told me to use protection if I was to do this, and said she didn't want to know anything more about it. She actually seemed pissed off but, having asked for this situation, could hardly renege on our deal. From what she'd told me, Cat hadn't had intercourse with Mark (or anyone else, for that matter), oral or otherwise, since starting down the D/s path. I had to believe her. But if she had wanted to, and had asked for my thoughts, how would I have reacted? I imagine I would have been absolutely enraged at the idea, but would finally have acquiesced, and been miserable about it from then onwards. Regardless, I had the go-ahead. I just wasn't sure I could actually go ahead with anything.

Back in the bedroom that day, Faith told me she wanted me in her; that she was simply too horny, and couldn't possibly hold on any longer. I told her to get onto all fours on the bed. She did so, spreading her legs, invitingly. I was erect, I was excited, I was horny as hell, but I couldn't go through with it. Instead I slapped Faith – hard – on her arse. I had never spanked her properly before now. I'd tied her up a lot, used various items to caress her, brought her to orgasm with my hands, even pinched her nipples and labia, and slapped her softly with the ruler a few times on her breasts and her pussy. But no real spanking. So when I did this now, she squealed and jumped, turning to glare at me, and yelled, 'What the fuck was that?' I stood beside her with my arms folded, trousers zipped up (hopefully covered by my T-shirt and so not displaying my desire), and told her that D/s included the use of spanking to punish acts of insubordination. It was all I could think of. I told her that she'd been naughty for wanting sex so badly, and that I was the one in charge. I packed my things and left, catching a glimpse of Faith as I walked out of the bedroom. She looked furious.

That was the last time I saw her, aside from a few awkward school runs where we tried to avoid each other. She texted me to say that she didn't appreciate being led on, and was fed up with the whole D/s thing. She told me that what we did had been fun but she wanted more, and if I wasn't up for it then I should just fuck off. So I fucked off. Seems Faith wasn't naturally inclined towards D/s. Hell, nor am I, but at least I'd tried. And, by God, it was amazing.

That was last week, and today I'm sitting here writing, bored, and with nothing better to do. Did I go about things the wrong way? Did I hurt or insult Faith because I didn't want to be unfaithful to Cat? Maybe it was because I wanted to retain the moral high ground, somehow. Was I subconsciously trying to save Faith from potentially getting hurt emotionally? Or was I just not man enough to tackle the situation when it came to the crunch? I guess I'll never know.

Author's note

This is where my imagined storyline ended. I had planned to finish it off with some description of how happy Cat and I were in our current situation, and how our lives were falling into some sort of normal routine in which we both played on occasion, but overall life was good and things were continuing as they had before Cat's revelation – albeit with a bit of kinky fun thrown in every now and again.

While I was composing this chapter, I'd also been writing separate entries about my real life. I was still upset by the fact that Cat was interacting with someone else, and that there was obvious tension between us. I had tried my damnedest to make things work, had done everything I could possibly think of to save my marriage, yet it still seemed to be heading inexorably downhill.

Having written this fantasy, it dawned on me that maybe what I needed was a submissive of my own. But, how to find one? The BDSM world still scared the hell out of me; I knew almost nothing about being a Dom, much less how to become involved in the actual lifestyle. (Although calling it a lifestyle, a community, or a scene is frowned upon by some. God knows what to call it, then; I'll stick with what I know for now). And so I read and researched a bit more. I discovered that the best way to start meeting other members of the community, and to become familiar with the scene, was to attend something called a "munch"; a gathering of kinksters at a local venue, where drinks and stories are enjoyed. Most munches take place regularly, and are generally suited to individuals based on location or a particular kink preference.

While the reality that followed wasn't quite as glamorous as I'd imagined, it turned out to be a damn sight more interesting.

Part Six
Back to Life, Back to (a new) Reality

22 September 2010

Today I attended my first munch. This is an event where deviants meet to eat, drink, and talk at a mutually convenient local venue. I signed up to a brilliant BDSM and kink website where people can post pictures, write stories, or ask questions and participate in discussions on a forum. I was initially pretty apprehensive about it, especially looking at some of the images and articles posted. Needles seem rather popular, and I seriously don't understand the attraction to that sort of thing. What am I getting into here?

Anyway, I've spent a while on the website and it's incredibly informative. I've also chatted to some very friendly people who are local to me, and who recommended that I attend a munch or event in the area in order to meet like-minded folk and discuss kink.

A few of the people I've been chatting to have directed me to a local group who meet monthly. I've joined the group and have read a lot of posts, and they all seem pretty decent. They haven't been going for very long – only a few months, apparently. The group was established after a few of the members had a falling-out with a much larger group based in the city. Political tension exists in every corner of life, I guess. These guys hold a munch at a pub about ten miles from here. Apparently, it has a secluded seating area behind the main bar, so that they can chat without earning too many wayward glares from passers-by should the conversation get rowdy. I've introduced myself on the forum, so let's see what happens. I'm wondering if I'll go through with actually meeting these people some time.

5 October 2010

Not much news since the last entry. A few people have commented on my post, mostly welcoming me and offering advice to a newbie. Their October munch is happening tomorrow night and I've listed myself as attending. I'm shitting myself.

7 October 2010

I munched! And, unsurprisingly, survived to tell the tale. Not very much to report, though, in truth. I arrived at the pub early, and found three pretty normal-looking people sitting at a large table, which had a small stuffed toy on it to help identify the group to newcomers; this is apparently standard practice. Even so, I wasn't terribly sure what to do or say, and was nervous even as I approached the table. I introduced myself and was greeted very warmly, first by the munch organiser – who has a photo of herself on the website for easy recognition – and then by the rest of them. After that, I just sort of sat there and sipped my pint of ale while I listened to them talking, and they asked me a few questions about my life. I was really nervous and wasn't sure exactly how much to reveal, so I tried to be a bit elusive without being offensive; a tricky balance. I hoped it was OK and that they all just thought I was shy. One particular person, a lovely fellow called Tony, engaged me in conversation. I recognised him as someone I've chatted to a few times online, and who has been really helpful and friendly in all his messages. Tony was the first person to reach out to me, to welcome me to the community and to reassure me that I had nothing to fear so long as I remained true to myself. Tony is an "old school" Dom, and he's been involved in BDSM for a long time. I knew he'd be here and I was extremely nervous about meeting him. Turns out he's just a regular guy. Who woulda thunk it, eh?

Tony and I chatted quite a bit, but the others were also very friendly and pleasant. As the evening progressed others joined us and I was introduced – not that there's a hope in hell I'll remember anyone's name aside from Tony and the organiser, MistressD (whose real name is Jess, and she's far less intimidating in real life than online!). The next few hours were filled with discussions on very normal everyday things like cars, photography, and music. And occasionally, kink. My curiosity encouraged me to ask questions, and my new friends seemed happy to answer them. As I sat there listening, it occurred to me that the kink community was probably not so very different from the rest of society. These people were lovely, warm, intelligent human beings, who just happened to enjoy an alternative way of expressing intimacy. Why, then, is BDSM so vilified by the vanilla world? Decades of negative publicity and misinformation, that's why.

Tony had to leave for a night shift, which was a pity because I'd been enjoying talking to him. His insight into the murky world of kink was fascinating. Soon after he left, a couple called Andy and Sue arrived. More enlightening conversation and easy banter ensued, and we drank coffee late into the night.

8 October 2010

The munch was great, and I loved every minute of it. I've already signed up for the next one. I've accepted online friend requests from all of the attendees at the last one, as well as various other members of the group. Exciting times.

17 October 2010

Haven't been writing much lately. I've been too busy with my new friends, and with reading and exploring online. There's a lot of useful information, but the one thing I have read consistently is that, to actually live the lifestyle, you need to get out there and meet people. And I'm doing just that. Yay, me!

12 November 2010

The second munch was brilliant, yet again, and I've made a lovely new friend.

Tony couldn't make it, which disappointed me initially. Fortunately, though, everyone else made me feel completely welcome and relaxed again. There was a new face there; someone who is apparently a regular but who was away and couldn't make the previous meet. She's a delightful lady with whom I'd had a few enlightening conversations online. Her name is Laura. She is a Domme, and she has opened my eyes to many interesting and exciting prospects. The munch wasn't terribly well attended, compared to last time, and most of the attendees left fairly early. Laura and I shifted to a smaller table in a corner and drank coffee, discussing (rather loudly, but nobody seemed to notice) the joys of rope use and bondage.

23 November 2010

I've been a busy boy. I've visited Laura at her apartment a few times now, as well as enjoying a few cups of tea at Tony's place. That these relative strangers have invited me into their homes is a testament to the trust they place in me. I'm touched by their openness, and their willingness to spend their free time teaching a complete newbie the ropes (as it were). Not a stitch of clothing has been removed during any of these visits, yet I have been instructed as to safety techniques and procedures when using rope. I've also learned a lot about different types of restraints, and some very interesting uses for everyday household items. Both of my new friends have a wealth of knowledge to share. Laura has a man in her life who she subs to, even though she is a professional Domme. It's one of many confusing aspects within this strange and wonderful new world I've discovered. When I mentioned this to Laura, she pointed me in the direction of numerous books about BDSM, which could prove useful or entertaining. Or both, ideally.

24 November 2010

The next munch has been announced on the website. We're trying a different pub this time. The previous one had, until recently, been a fantastically welcoming old place in the countryside, but has now become a "gastropub" under pretentious new management. This gastropub (like many others popping up around here, so Laura tells me) focuses on fine food, and encourages patrons to spend vast amounts of money dining. We don't need that. We need an open and informal environment in which to meet and discuss kink, amongst other things. And if a pint and a meal happen to be available for consumption, then so be it. I notice I'm using the term "we", like I'm a bona fide part of this community now. An old hand, well versed in all things kinky. Ha! I love it.

12 December 2010

Yet another success. Why could anyone possibly be daunted by the idea of attending a munch? You get to meet like-minded, friendly people who are more than happy to talk to everyone present about pretty much any topic under the sun.

This munch held a pleasant surprise in store, in the form of a lady called Alice. She had sent me a simple message via the website, a while ago, saying, *just wanted to say hi, as a mutual friend speaks highly of you and i'm hoping to meet you at the next munch*. I noted the lack of capitalisation, a potential sign of submissiveness (or possibly grammatical ignorance, but I was hoping for the former). I replied, thanking her for her message. We sent a few more emails back and forth over the next couple of days; chatty rather than flirty, but there was something in our exchanges that left me with a sense of anticipation. It was nothing explicit but, somehow, the overall tone hinted at the prospect of something new, something potentially exciting. The day before the event, I sent Alice one last message, telling her I was looking forward to meeting. I didn't want to get my hopes up that anything might happen, but as I was driving to the munch I suddenly realised that I had a huge, stupid grin all over my face.

The munch itself was slightly larger than the previous ones; seventeen attendees in total. I was sitting at the table, chatting to Tony and Laura, when Alice arrived. She was with her friends, Andy and Sue, who had been at that first munch I'd attended but not the second one. Alice was stunning; tall and slim with long blonde hair, and dressed in a delightful Gothy-looking outfit and stiletto boots. I spent the rest of my night glancing at her (surreptitiously, I hoped) as I socialised with my other new friends. Alice seemed enamoured with the group's little soft toy – a red and white striped zebra. I was hoping she was equally enamoured with me; I did catch her throwing an occasional glance my way, but maybe she was just being polite by smiling at my lack of social graces and awkward conversational skills. The group spent a thoroughly enjoyable few hours chatting and drinking (mainly coffee). As it grew later and everyone started leaving, Andy suggested that the four of us – himself, Sue, Alice and I – head over to their place which was a short distance away, and enjoy a nightcap or a cup of something there, instead. Sue suggested that Alice could accompany me in my car, to "show me the way".

Once we got to the car, Alice bashfully confessed that she had no idea where to go. She'd been to the house before, so would recognise it once we got close. We talked as I drove, randomly turning into driveways and then backing out again, but not caring very much at all. We finally found the house, but elected to stay in the car for a while longer. I asked Alice what she was thinking. She paused, briefly, and then said that she wanted me to grab her ponytail and pull her head back, hard, and kiss her. It would have been impolite to decline, so I did what any gentleman would have done, and obliged.

I was initially very aware that this was the first woman I'd kissed since meeting Catherine, and it felt slightly awkward. An imagined scenario is far from the reality of a situation. My emotions were kicking me in the head from every direction. But I decided that, as Cat had started this, and since she was enjoying herself with other play partners, I sure as hell could do so, too.

When we finally got into the house, Andy and Sue were preparing some cups and boiling the kettle. They both had sly smiles on their faces as we shuffled in. For the next two hours, we all chatted and enjoyed numerous cups of tea. Andy eventually declared that he was off to bed and so I stood up, ready to leave. As I did, Andy offered Alice and me the use of a spare room, and Sue told me she would gather a few of their favourite toys for us to enjoy. Stay the night? What toys? And what the hell was I supposed to do with them, anyway? Things were suddenly moving considerably faster than I'd anticipated. I glanced at Alice with an expression that I hoped didn't give away my surprise or excitement. She was staring back at me with an uncertain look on her face. I shrugged and smiled, and managed to utter something like, 'Cool.'

Sue and Alice headed off to find the toys, as I stood gazing blankly at various paintings on the wall. I was spinning. I'd only just met Alice, and now I was supposed to … what? Hit her with something? Put my hands all over her? God, *undress* her? I didn't have a clue what I was doing, or why I was still here. All I wanted to do was run away. Maybe.

But then I thought about Catherine, again; about how she had wanted this for me, had wanted me to make friends and enjoy myself, much like she was enjoying herself in this newfound lifestyle. Why should I feel guilty? Why should I not have a fantastic evening with another human being, just as Cat was happily doing from time to time? I relaxed, somewhat, although the idea of having to "perform" on a real, live, not-online submissive – one with hopes and expectations of what I could do for her – was ridiculously intimidating. I texted Cat to say I'd be away all night (we had discussed a while ago that this sort of thing could be a possibility, so I didn't feel too bad about it), received a somehow disappointing, *OK, see you tomorrow* response, and switched my phone off.

Alice returned to the living room, took my hand,

and led me to the spare bedroom. My heart was racing. The bed was arrayed with a variety of goodies, and – thank the fucking stars – I recognised a few of them; pinwheel, flogger, rope, and PVC tape. I asked Alice to remove her stilettos. Then – showing no originality, but I couldn't think of what else to do – I pulled her hair back again and kissed her. I was less reserved this time, and my senses were a lot sharper since I'd decided to relax and enjoy myself. I felt Alice's tension in her rigid pose, as well as noting her rapid breathing and soft moans as my tongue explored her mouth. The excitement that these sensations stirred in me is something I will remember for a very long time. They are what made me realise that, actually, maybe I could get used to this whole BDSM business after all. Following that kiss, everything seemed so much easier. I told Alice to lie back on the bed and, after she had very quickly complied, I grabbed her trousers and pulled them down and off her amazingly long legs. Then I told her to turn over. I bound her wrists behind her back with PVC tape. I sat on top of her and ran my hands over her body, gently. I was still fully clothed. She was breathing hard when I climbed off. I reached for the flogger, and set to work, gently whipping her shoulders, upper back, and buttocks. I stopped occasionally, rubbing my hands over her back and thighs, and then continuing with the flogging, each stroke slightly harder than the last. After doing this for about five minutes, I stopped and removed her panties.

Although we hadn't discussed any of the subjects mentioned in various "how to" books on BDSM, such as likes, dislikes and limits, I had, at least, mentioned before we started playing that Alice needed to tell me what her safe word was. She'd settled on "red", a commonly used distress call during kinky play scenarios. I reminded her that she needed to use it if, at any point, I was doing something she couldn't handle.

Having a gorgeous woman, someone I'd just met, lying face down on a bed in front of me with her hands tied and her naked backside exposed was one of the biggest thrills I've ever experienced. I was incredibly hard, but had to maintain my composure. My role as a Dom is to please my submissive, first and foremost. And I was determined to get that part right. I used the pinwheel on her, running it down her thighs, inside and out, but avoiding getting anywhere near her pussy (which was, by this time, a gleaming, dripping, amazingly inviting, juicy mess). Alice jerked and squealed as the sharp points pricked her skin. I used my hand to trace over the path of the wheel, bringing my fingers as close as possible to Alice's vagina without actually touching it. She was squirming by this stage. I told her to get onto her knees, something not easily done with your hands bound behind you, but she managed it admirably. When she was kneeling, I removed the tape from her wrists, ordered her to put on a blindfold, and then positioned her; head on the bed, backside in the air, and arms to either side of her body. I used the rope, one end tied to each wrist, and then down and underneath the bed. This is an extremely vulnerable position, and I asked her if she was still all right. She whispered (actually, that's generous; she croaked) that she was fine.

I ran my hands over the back of her neck, grabbing her hair as I progressed up her back. I stroked her delicious bottom, and then moved across the back of her thighs. Alice was wriggling, which got worse as I moved to the inside of her legs. I positioned myself on the bed beside her, slowly caressing her hips and backside, occasionally roaming across her stomach. And then I stopped. This is where a blindfold comes in handy; she had no idea why I'd stopped, or what I was doing. I got off the bed, removed my shirt and socks, and rummaged through a few of the toys. Sensation is everything in this sort of scene, and the fact that she could hear, but not see, what I was doing was, hopefully, driving Alice insane. I stood beside her for a further five minutes or so, and observed – delightedly – that her pussy was still incredibly moist. For my part, I hadn't lost my erection for the past half an hour. I leaned forward and shoved my thumb into her, hard. Alice shot forward, with a loud moan. I'd anticipated some sort of strong reaction, so I kept a grip on her shoulders with my other hand, shoving her back into position again and holding my thumb in place. I ran my forefinger up and down her labia. Then I removed my thumb, and told Alice to keep still. I used my left hand to hold her open while my right index finger slowly and gently found her clitoris. Alice was almost uncontrollably moaning and pushing against me by now, and the feeling of power and eroticism I felt at that point is, I think, what makes Dominants do what they do. It's indescribable.

I continued toying with Alice's clit for a while longer, occasionally dipping my fingers into her. And then she surprised me by asking whether she was allowed to come. I stopped what I was doing momentarily while I considered this. Alice groaned. She was asking for my permission to do something I hadn't even realised would be within my control; I'd just sort of assumed she'd have an orgasm, and that would be that. Yet another sign that I was with a true submissive, and someone who had handed her trust over to me, absolutely. I replied, 'Not yet,' and pushed my fingers into her again. Thank God for the blindfold – I was smiling like a bloody fool, mostly at the fact that I was actually doing this, and it was working.

I could have continued playing with Alice all night long, but I didn't want to overdo it; that would have exposed me as the complete amateur I am, which would have sucked. Even though I'd made no secret of my limited experience in BDSM, and Alice was aware of how new I was at this, I had to at least make an effort to get this right. I started moving my hands over her body again, and then went back to massaging her clit and fingering her ridiculously wet pussy. And, when Alice next begged me to be allowed to come, I let her.

13 December 2010

I woke up at 10 a.m. with Alice curled up beside me, my arms around her. Waking up with an unfamiliar face next to mine was a strange experience, but not as awkward as I'd imagined. I could get to enjoy this.

We had breakfast and coffee with Andy and Sue, and then went our separate ways. Our hosts are such lovely people, and I can see myself becoming good friends with them. Or rather, Alice and I becoming good friends with them, as a couple. Now *that's* a surreal thought.

I'd enjoyed my evening immensely, as had Alice. We've been chatting online since I got home. I have a wife, but I'm "dating" someone else, with my wife's consent. This feels so fucking weird!

17 December 2010

I've been ignoring you, diary. So sorry. Other things on the go, you understand. I'll update as and when I get a chance.

22 December 2010

Alice and I joined Andy and Sue at a fetish club in London – our first proper event! It was very similar to clubs I've frequented in Brazil, in that it was dark and gloomy, and full of people wearing bizarre outfits. So, not much of a shock, really. Once inside the club, people's clothes started coming off, or being replaced with other outfits ranging from PVC to leather, to full latex ensembles. I don't get the appeal of dressing up, but who knows? It may well end up becoming a fetish favourite of ours, somewhere down the line.

As we walked away from the dance area and entered the play room on the side, we were approached by a friendly, moustachioed man with a belt full of whips and strange-looking devices. I was curious about his collection and we chatted for a while regarding their use, after which he offered to teach me various techniques. I, in turn, was happy to provide him with a slightly nervous submissive to demonstrate on. Having Alice hike her skirt up to expose her thong-clad bottom to a room full of strangers was an odd experience, but one that seemed to work for both of us. Mr Whippy (never did catch his name) showed me how to use some of his toys, and Alice was left with a nicely warmed bottom by the end of it. I truly do not get why a sore arse is a good thing, but I hope to find out sometime; hopefully not by having my own arse whipped, though.

I have so much to learn, as our evening out taught me. We witnessed someone using a bullwhip – have to get myself one of those, they're so cool! – and rope suspension. Again, the latter not being something I see the point of, but apparently people love getting suspended. My friend, Laura, has explained a few things to me, along the lines of having someone else in control of your mind and your body, of allowing them to govern your movement, so I'm guessing that's the deal. But the thrill of it is what I don't understand. I really must try rope with Alice sometime. Not suspension, though – I'd need to be bloody confident before doing anything involving pressure points and potentially cutting off blood supply with badly thought-out knots and ties. It's not a beginner's game.

13 February 2011

Time has passed. It passes so quickly, these days. I've been seeing Alice, on average, around twice a month, as well as occasionally for coffee on a Tuesday morning, when she sees a client in the area. I still attend the munches, which are wonderfully social and fun, and also pretty informative. But these days I don't arrive alone. Alice is amazing. She's sexy, intelligent, and very funny. We're discovering that we have a lot more in common than just kink. Although that side of it is pretty damn good. Alice has started inviting me to her house, which is another sign of trust. Trust is integral in any relationship and, I'd guess, especially so in a D/s one. Alice is separated from her husband, who is living with another woman, so we have a house all to ourselves. Smacks of something I wrote a while back in my imagined scenarios. We're slowly trying new things, although we keep coming back to the basics; a bit of bondage, some spanking, some discipline (hair-pulling, orders to stand facing a corner, kneeling on a hard surface, collecting a paddle in order to have smacks administered, and so on). We've tried playing with wax, too, which is fun but messy. Plastic sheets are a must. Thanks, Laura, for yet more excellent advice.

16 February 2011

Alice has been begging to give me a blow job. I've been hiding behind the excuse, 'It's my duty as a good Dom to not allow this,' but, in reality, I was just afraid that the dynamic would change; that I'd be moving away from the relative safety of playing with someone to becoming sexually active with a new partner. I raised the point with Cat, a while ago, and she seemed absolutely fine with it. On the proviso that I was careful. Whatever that means. Aside from wearing a condom, how is anyone ever "careful" having a relationship outside of marriage? Yes, the prospect of having a new sexual partner is exciting and sexy as hell. I like the idea, but it's not the point around which my entire existence revolves. And if I want sex, then I can have it with Catherine. We still do that, on occasion.

All of this is fucking with my head. I am so out of my comfort zone, here. Does it count as being unfaithful if your wife has actually given you her blessing? Doesn't seem that way, and yet … Christ. I don't know what to think, any more.

24 February 2011

I gave in. We were having the most incredible scene. I had bound Alice with rope and used a paddle to warm up her backside, and then grabbed a handful of her hair and pulled her head back, and shoved my tongue down her throat. She reeled back after that, and started begging me, yet again, to suck my cock. I decided that it would be rude to keep refusing this woman; this panting, horny submissive who wanted nothing more than to please me. So I let her run her hands all over me, loosen my jeans, and pleasure me with her mouth. Her enthusiasm was clear, and her endurance was admirable. Mine, less so. It was, quite simply, beautiful.

7 March 2011

Alice and I have incorporated full-penetration sex into our play sessions. Using condoms. I guess I knew it wouldn't be a giant leap from oral to other areas. I've heard and read varying – often conflicting – reports about sex within a D/s relationship. Many people are appalled at the idea, yet others state that the whole premise of kink is based around sex and orgasm. I tend to favour the latter, not only because I enjoy sex (let's face it, as a species we'd be doomed if nobody enjoyed doing it), but also because playing with another naked human being is extremely intimate. As a Dom, you have essentially been given permission to control the mind and body of another person. As a teenager, I'd often dream about being a woman for a day, and being able to stare at myself in a mirror, or touch myself. It was a very exciting fantasy, and one which I'm sure many teenage boys share. And now, having been gifted a female body to do with as I please, having a beautiful woman willingly relinquish herself entirely into my hands, I find myself in a most enviable position. I can't believe I'm living this life. This is something so far removed from where I ever thought I'd be at my age. Cat, with her "coming out", has pushed me into confronting my midlife crisis before it actually happens. But, instead of buying a sports car, I'm undressing and doing unspeakable things to what amounts to a girlfriend, but with the consent of my wife. Who in their right mind wouldn't want this?

23 March 2011

I owe Alice so much for helping me make my transition from nervous newbie to confident Dominant. Alice is intelligent, sensual and funny, and has a wicked twinkle in her eyes. She has placed her trust in me and allowed me to see her as she really is; no façade, no having to conform to what society expects from a professional woman in her forties, no bullshit, or lies, or falsehood in order to secure me as a potential husband. She wants me to fulfil her fantasies, her deepest desires that she has kept bottled up inside her since she was a small child. And I will do that for her. Why? Because it turns me on. Simple as that. Giving her pleasure, observing as she squirms and moans from my touch, feeling her convulse as my actions bring her to climax – that's what it's all about. Am I a natural Dominant? Fuck no. But that doesn't mean I can't enjoy myself while I learn to become one.

25 March 2011

I remember writing, a while back, about how I wished I'd discovered this D/s thing when I was a teenager, or even in my twenties. But the more I live this lifestyle now, the more I'm coming to realise that it's not a young man's game. Certainly not if you expect to conduct yourself as a fairly competent and half-decent Dom. Experience, in this case, would seem to outweigh youthful exuberance. I'm having a really unexpected adventure in my life, and I'm enjoying myself a great deal.

19 April 2011

Tensions have been running high in our household for the past few weeks. Hence why I haven't written anything. I'm completely fucking miserable about the fact that Catherine is having physical dealings with Simon. Their arrangement has become a regular event, like she's going to a bi-monthly yoga session or something. Every meeting is even written on the kitchen calendar, for fuck's sake! Every time she heads out for an afternoon with her Dom, it eats away at me a little bit more. I have to put on a brave face, because this is what we've agreed upon, but there is no way in hell it feels OK to me. The fact that she's meeting another man is bad enough, but the knowledge that I'm, yet again, being left to sort out the kids is fucking galling in the extreme. If she was home every night and helped with the boys' routine, then I'm convinced this would feel less like a kick in the teeth. Or maybe not. God knows. But the knowledge that I could be having a night off to go out with mates or whatever, and instead she's out sucking some other guy's cock ... Jesus, I feel fucking homicidal just thinking about it. Yes, I realise how hypocritical this sounds, coming from someone who has very recently written about the amazing sex he's having with another woman. But I didn't start this. The D/s thing is not what I ever envisaged as being a part of my lifestyle; it's not how I ever wanted to live.

A few years ago I never knew any of this even existed. Could I switch off the D/s stuff tomorrow and go back to being a vanilla boy living in a vanilla world? I believe that I could. But Catherine can't do that. This is a part of who she is, and this is her world now – she can never go back. That knowledge scares me, and makes me worry for our future together.

26 April 2011

Every time Cat arrives home from work, every time I hear her car pull in, my heart skips a little beat. I still love that woman, and I experience a brief second of butterflies in my stomach before dread sets in, and my stress levels skyrocket. As she enters the house, James kicks off. We have some brilliant times together, yet at the sound of Cat's key in the door, it's like some binary switch is triggered and he turns from "lovely little boy" into "disgusting shitbag". Suddenly every rule is abandoned and all evidence of common sense disappears. And why? Because he knows that I will stop disciplining him the moment Cat gets home. He sees this as a weakness, and he exploits it. And you know what? Good on him. That skill will get him far in life. But for now his behaviour still makes me want to strangle the little bastard. He's too young to understand what he's doing to us, or to comprehend the tension this behaviour is causing. So I keep quiet, as far as possible. All I'm trying to do is keep the peace, and hold my marriage together for that much longer. But, for the past month or so, the tension has been increasing, and the divide between Cat and I grows ever wider. She and I hardly talk any more.

We're both trying, very obviously, to retain a level of normality that has always existed, in order to let the children think everything's fine. But everything is not fine. Everything is very far from being fine. I dread to think how this will end.

30 April 2011

I tried to get Cat to talk to me tonight. She told me she was too tired, and this wasn't the right time. So when, exactly, will be the right time? When it suits her, that's when. And I can guarantee that whenever that is, it won't be any time that suits me.

11 May 2011

I wrote a long letter to Catherine today. It outlined my thoughts and my feelings over the past few months. I went into a lot of detail about why exactly I've been so distant. I explained that my actions had been reciprocal, and that the extent of my unhappiness was directly related to the escalating closeness between her and Simon. I never sent the letter, of course. Why? I have no idea. What have I got to lose? My marriage? That's already lost. I can feel it in my bones. But even in a situation that I know has turned to shit, there has to be a slim chance that we can still fix this. So, while even the remotest possibility exists that we can stay together and watch our children grow, I have to hang onto that scrap of hope. What other option do I have?

23 May 2011

We had an absolutely brilliant munch last night. As we've done a few times, now, I met Alice at the venue an hour prior to the munch starting. We talked a bit about what's been happening at home. Alice surprised me. She completely wants Cat and I to sort our shit out, and retain a strong marriage for the sake of the children. Alice has become so much more to me than just a sub; she's been a pillar of support since the very beginning, and is constantly encouraging me to do what's right for me, and for the children's future stability. She completely understands why I'm stressed out. She's a good woman, and a good friend. Worst-case scenario would be that Cat and I split up. And if that happened ... well, it wouldn't really be a worst-case scenario at all, really. I doubt I'd feel the same if I didn't have Alice in my life.

But yeah, the munch. Thirty-nine people. Thirty-nine! I can't imagine how intimidating these numbers would have been if this was my first time but, having become a regular at the gatherings, it's really cool to be meeting new people. And, of course, seeing all of our old friends, too. "Old" seems a relative term these days; I've known most of these guys for such a short period, yet we've already established very firm friendships. We all talked late into the night, and were eventually asked to leave by a miserable, long-faced waitress with a shitty attitude. But, otherwise, a great evening, and one that I am definitely looking forward to repeating next month. Albeit, perhaps, at a different venue.

28 May 2011

Catherine's mother is coming to stay with us. Again. Jesus! Every time we get more than two days together as a family, her bloody mother suddenly appears. It's like Cat doesn't actually want to spend any time with the rest of us, unchaperoned. So – just in case tensions weren't already running high enough – we now have this added fun factor. I'm truly fucking overjoyed.

13 July 2011

Mother-in-law came and went. Two lovely, fun-filled weeks of her feeding the children crap while I battled to get them to eat vegetables instead. Great stuff. I do love her little visits. And timing-wise, it couldn't have been better. I think she picked up on day one that there was a razor wire between Cat and me. Yet she didn't say anything; didn't even offer us a night out to talk through stuff while she watched the boys. Insightful, *non*? But then, she had an affair and her husband stayed with her, so I guess it's what passes for normal in her life. What's wrong with us menfolk? Why can't we be the stereotypical beefcake alpha male bullies who treat their women like shit? Being caring, gentle, and considerate earns us a fucking slap, so you'd think we would have realised by now that we need to act differently. Ironically, Cat's sister, whose husband treats her like dirt, is very much in love and dedicated to her man. What a strange little world we live in.

28 July 2011

I need to get out. I've had enough of this rubbish. I got an earful from Cat earlier because I yelled at James to go to his room. Of course, he ran straight to his mum and cried into her skirt, and she stormed in demanding to know what was going on. He'd only punched his brother in the face. Silly me for even thinking he'd need to be punished, eh? I did something I haven't done before – I left the kids with her and walked down to the village pub. I enjoyed a pint and some time to myself. God knows why I haven't done that before now. We know one couple where the husband has done this every night, for the past decade; the wife hates it, but she adores him. God, I wish I'd been more of a cunt my entire life – I might actually command some respect, and have a stable marriage, if I'd done so.

I got home earlier and the lights were all out. I decided to sit at the computer and write this instead of getting into bed immediately. If Cat had still been awake, or said anything, it could have led to some unpleasantness. Or, God forbid, we might have been forced to actually discuss what's going on.

**Part Seven
Dear What the Fuck?**

31 July 2011

Jesus, talk about shit hitting the fan!

Catherine arrived home early last night, looking anxious. She told me she'd arranged for the kids to have a sleepover with friends across the road. When I asked why, Cat told me we needed to talk. Brilliant. I hadn't prepared a thing. But a part of me felt massively relieved; this was the confrontation we've needed to have for the past God knows how long.

I had all sorts of things I wanted to say, but Catherine, typically, hijacked everything. Instead of talking, she had prepared a bloody essay, which she emailed to me just after the kids had left the house. She told me to read it while she went upstairs to enjoy a long soak in the bath.

Here's what she wrote.

This letter has been months in the mental writing, and I've found it incredibly hard to get to the point of being able to put all this into words. I still don't feel ready to write it, but I know I need to, because I can't carry on like this and I don't think you can, either. I know I am going to cause hurt, and that's a big part of why I have endlessly put off saying this. The last thing I want is to be hurting you, but I fully realise that I have (and am) hurting you anyway, even by saying nothing ... And I am hurting, too, and I need to feel I am doing something about it. So here goes.

The things that I'm saying now have been spinning in circles in my head for so long, and I honestly don't know how to go about fixing it. I keep coming up against the same dead ends. So I'm going start the talking process and hope I can be honest, and hope you can, too.

I think we are broken. I know the obvious stuff from the last two years has been the immediate catalyst, and I realise you may think that's the whole problem. (Although I'm not really sure what you think at the moment, and I know you don't know what I think, so I'm sorry if I'm wrong in saying that.) And of course what I've done over the last two years has been a crisis for both of us, and has been bloody difficult. I'm not denying that. But I am reaching a point where I'm feeling silenced by having lost the moral high ground so spectacularly, and it means I've been accepting all the guilt and responsibility for us, and so I've felt unable to tell you that I am not happy for other reasons. So now I'm saying yes, I have caused untold stress and unhappiness for you, and I fully take responsibility for that. I hate that I have hurt you at all, let alone shattered you so badly – I love you so very much and I never set out to make you unhappy. But I am also stating now that there are reasons I am not happy, and I need to say them so that we can talk properly. A lot of the things I am going to say feel like very unkind comments, and I have truly deliberated for a long time about whether I have any right to say these things, but I have to hand back some of this stuff to you – I'm carrying it all now, and it's breaking me.

I am frustrated that you haven't wanted to work for so long. I'd foreseen the end of your employment at your previous company for years before it happened, because you were coasting. I know that you realised this, too, because you told me so on a few occasions. I remember having many conversations with you about what your plan was to keep yourself employable, but I couldn't make it happen for you. I think we both realise now that you aren't really employable in your old line of work, because your skills are so out of date– that frustrates me enormously, because I have been trying to get you to do something about that for years. I also regret the decisions we took together which made it seem like I'm fine with you not working. If you aren't going to work in IT again, what are you wanting to do? If it's writing, then where's the writing going? I can't see that you're making much effort at expanding your skills or ability. But for writing to be a serious employable endeavour it takes a lot of effort, not occasional spurts of work. I know you'll say that you're too busy looking after the kids and the house, but you have hours to yourself every day, and I've said repeatedly that housework isn't a priority. And if we're honest, other than dishes and clothes loads, housework happens quite occasionally as a total event, which is fine by me. But it's not something you're spending every minute on. It seems and feels now like you're quite happy to coast doing nothing – I know that sounds incredibly harsh, but is it wrong?

I am working stupid hours, and I know that is a major problem, too – I'm an absent wife and parent a lot of the time. It feels like you've been OK for me to do that, though, and to add in extra tutoring to keep somewhere near financial coping (which we aren't), so that you're not having to work. This is just what I do: I am an education professional. It takes a lot of work and a lot of time. It's not going to change – it really worries me that you think everything will suddenly get easier when I qualify for a senior post. Yes, life will be more predictable, but the hours and the extracurricular work will always be there.

Financially we are in a mess. It has been an endless worry for a few years now, and I can't fix it any more. I am not prepared to be doing so many extra hours any more – I don't see much of my kids, and get so few down days. I have tried my absolute bloody hardest to shield you from this, because I've been concerned about making you feel bad about it. But the reality is that I'm carrying too much here – we both have a responsibility to keep us financially stable. Since your job went we have been paying for James to be in preschool so that you could have downtime and head space – the full days twice a week at his previous nursery school cost us an absolute fortune. I can't see that you used that time for anything. It seemed to be a way to get you distance from James, and you were always very outspoken about not wanting him at home with you all the time, which I have found very hard to hear. I have had to renegotiate the mortgage, so we have very little equity on the house now. I have taken on extra work, but I can't be the only one doing anything about it any more. I guess this part of my letter is the easier one to solve: you need to be doing something towards earning again. I have said repeatedly that I don't mind that you have not earned for the last three years, but I have thought it important to be skilling up or learning something while you're at home, so that there's an end to this situation.

At home, I am really unhappy. I feel like I have little say in what goes on, because you have such a vast list of rules and procedures, but I am not allowed to be with the boys without them. This has made me feel sidelined as a parent. When I'm with the kids alone, I can relate to them on my own terms without constraints, and I love that time so much. I know you say you love the time you have with them, and they clearly love it, too. So it's me who's not fitting in, and that hurts a lot. I feel like I'm not at home much, they miss me, I'm full of guilt about that, and then when I am here I have to fit into rules which aren't mine, and which I find suffocating and pointless. I guess that's just how I am, and I can't change it, as much as you can't change your way of doing things. I find it very hard watching the struggle you and James have ... I know you love him deeply, and he clearly adores you. But from where I stand it looks like he gets a pretty harsh deal from you – you are hard on him. I know I can't control your relationship with him, and it's something the two of you will have to work through yourselves – but I worry that you blame him for so much of our stress and unhappiness. He is a kid. We are the adults in the situation, and it's our problem, not his. It makes me feel so protective of him, and I'm aware we're setting up a dynamic that makes my relationship with him too much the other way, which doesn't really help, either, and which is my problem to sort out. I often feel I have to either back you up (which I feel I should do to make us appear united) and watch him being quite harshly admonished, or intervene on his behalf (a very strong pull) and undermine your parenting. Either way I can't win, and I'm sick of it.

I have wondered if your lack of energy and lack of drive is depression-related. I was so glad when you finally agreed to go onto anti-depressants, and I saw a big difference in you, but I guess it all coincided with you getting some interests outside of the house, and I think that's probably been what's made the difference, more than medication. I was frustrated that you stopped them without telling me you were going to, but I have to admit that you seem better than you were earlier this year, even without meds, so maybe it's a non-issue.

I guess the trickiest stuff to talk about is what's going on with us as a couple, and the other people in our lives. My discovery of D/s last year was an accident in the sense that I stumbled onto the fact that there are so many other people who feel as I do and that there's an outlet for these impulses and ways of thinking – I didn't go looking for that. But I guess my decision to explore it and interact with people online last year wasn't an accident – I am craving a space where I don't have to be the one doing the planning and organising and controlling, or taking all the responsibility. My journey through this over the past two years has been so turbulent for me – it's been a difficult thing to integrate into my own head, and nearly impossible to integrate into my life in real terms. You have been great in trying to understand what's been going on in me, and I am so incredibly grateful for the way you've handled it. I guess the difficulty is that I am absolutely comfortable with my sub identity now, I know this is who I am, and I'm OK with it. I know it's never going to go away, and I have no intention of ever trying to live a lie again ... I am not going to give it up. I interacted with other Doms online last year in brief, sporadic spurts; nothing serious, but enough to know that in Simon I have found an amazing man. My relationship with him can't be any more than it is now, but he has become a very important part of my life.

Your venture into D/s has bewildered and worried and relieved me all at the same time. I'm really not sure I understand what you wanted from it when you started exploring. It felt like it was a competition with me for who could be the most open-minded and outrageous, but I think it's changed for you as you've met real people and interacted with them. I'm really not sure how big a part of your life this all is, and I don't need to know. I have to say that when you met Alice I was just so relieved: partly that you were finally getting out of the house and seeming interested in life again, and partly that it took the pressure off me – I felt a very heavy weight of responsibility for being everything for you (and then feeling I had shattered that responsibility by my interaction with a Dom). I guess the really difficult stuff for us now is this: when you first told me a while ago that you were meeting Alice and staying over, I thought perhaps I'd feel jealous, or realise how much I had hurt you, but what I feel when you go to spend time with her is relief. I love the space that I can have alone at home, with the boys on my terms. I love that you are having something positive and exciting in your life – I understand the buzz you're getting and I am genuinely happy that you're seeing her.

So what about us then? This is the really hard stuff.

I have been so completely careful not to let my D/s impact on our lives (not seen by friends, not seeing Simon on weekends, not exposing myself to unsafe sex etc. – I have had sex, very rarely, and protected, by the way ... just so we're all out in the open.) I'm so, so glad you told me about it when you had sex with Alice –

thank you for the honesty. My lack of anger or even hurt about it has surprised me to some extent: I honestly haven't minded what you do with Alice or anyone else. But I am aware that you and I are no longer being physical. I feel we had already drifted so far apart by the time this happened (for a multitude of reasons as I've tried to explain above), that I don't feel I've missed our physical relationship. I guess, also, I'm just not vanilla, and as you predicted and worried would happen (and I endlessly reassured you wouldn't happen), I am struggling to see how a vanilla sexual relationship works for me. I know how hard this will be for you to read – I wish it wasn't the case. But it is. I couldn't have predicted it, and maybe in different circumstances it wouldn't have happened like this. But it has ...

So what do we do now? I have put off having this conversation with you for a long time (part of it for years ...). I have worried deeply that you'd react (as you might still) by saying that you're going back to Brazil, and that leaves the kids with one parent on each continent, and I felt previously that it would be my responsibility if it happened. There's no good time for this talk, but we're both so obviously strained now that we just have to get on with it, I think. I don't know the answers; we'll have to reach them by talking together. I have got to a point of genuinely not knowing what I want to do. I don't want to upend the boys' lives, and that has been a big part of me trying to keep this all inside and make everything fine. But I can't do it any more ... I'm not fine, I'm not happy, and I realise that things have to change. I can't envisage what our future might look like together anymore. I want to work hard; I want to have financial security and freedom to spend some cash on fun stuff and go on holidays and just live a little again. I know you seem to want the same, and you genuinely seem to think I can make that happen by myself.

Right now I think that I need a space to think about things from a slightly more detached and less angry position – I can't do that at home. So I'm suggesting we consider having some time apart in a way that protects the kids as much as we can, so that we can take stock of what's actually going on in our heads and our relationship. I don't know how the logistics could work, although I have some thoughts and ideas. I know you won't want this at all (or maybe you do, and I am just totally out of touch with what you're thinking). And I am so very sorry that it's got the point where I can't see a way forward without much more unhappiness for all of us. I don't want to see you hurt – in fact, what I want most is for both of us to be happy. But you have seemed miserable with life for so long. And right now I'm not happy, either, and that's not me, and I want to change it. By suggesting this I am not prejudging an outcome. I genuinely and deeply don't know what I want, but I just can't carry on like this. It's the only way I can think of to give us both space to think. Obviously the boys need protecting, but they also need a functional home, and I'm not sure they have that at the moment.

So can we start talking? I know our friends in the village will help with kids if we want time alone, and I think we'll have to use that. I don't relish the idea of these conversations at all – and I'm sure you don't either. I'm sorry.

I do love you, and that has always and will always be the case.

C

The first thing that struck me – left me reeling, in fact – was how, after all these months of agonising, after all these years of me trying to make things right by whatever means necessary – Catherine had found a way to turn this around and make *me* the villain. Really? The fucking gall of that woman!

OK, let's look at these issues I've so callously shoved in her face. Firstly, my controversial style of raising our children (in my youth it was called *discipline*; most families had it and weren't persecuted for doing it, and kids generally had a bit of respect and decency). The issue is pretty easily fixed, really. In fact, it could have completely evaporated at any time if I'd ever been made aware that it was such a catastrophic problem. And making it so would have taken all of about a minute of discussion, any time Cat had bothered to mention it. I am writing this a few days after these events took place and, since then, I have not once raised my voice or done anything to stop James from smacking Robert or throwing his dinner across the house. It really was that easy to solve.

On to the second issue: our dire financial position. Perhaps not so easily remedied, but very easily addressed. At the very least, it would have been worth talking about and thinking through a few options, if I'd been made aware of the seriousness of the situation. A recurring theme, it would seem. Cat and I had an agreement, struck up when I was made redundant. That agreement was for me to remain at home and look after the children, while Cat furthered her career. Note: *career*. I never had a career, nor would I have had in IT. I just had a job, and to further myself in that line would have meant doing the same thing at a different company. Yes, I could have studied other disciplines or new programs, but that all costs money, as does buying said programs to practice on at home. In the region of thousands of pounds, in some cases. I'll admit that the idea of sitting behind a desk for the rest of my life had lost its appeal. I wanted to write. But again, writing courses cost money, and time. What I did do was write in my spare time. Cat failed to understand that writing takes a lot of time, a lot of rereading, editing, and creativity. The creativity part was always the problem; inspiration tends to come when you least expect it, and not always on demand. There were times when I'd dedicate an entire morning to writing. But whenever I sat down, determined to produce something worthwhile, I'd inevitably find that just as I was starting to get properly stuck in, it would be time to collect a kid. Writing is not a career to pursue while running a household and looking after two children.

Third point: my depression. I think I probably was depressed. It seemed to coincide with me losing my job and discovering that Catherine was having an affair, oddly. I only started taking anti-depressants much later on, and then stopped again after I had met Alice and various others involved in the BDSM lifestyle.

And finally – least important, apparently, and featuring only marginally (almost to the point of insignificance) in Cat's essay – the situation with her and Simon, the man who she's been having an affair with, to all intents and purposes, for so long. This minor issue being the catalyst which kicked this all off and has been brewing into a fucking shit storm ever since. Yet, strangely, it seems hardly to be a factor at all in Cat's mind. How can she not see what's right in front of her two faces? I remember so many times, while we watched politics on the TV news, we'd comment about how ludicrously transparent all the corrupt politicians were in their attempts to bullshit the same public who had voted for them. They all lied and cast the blame elsewhere, all the while failing to realise that everyone could see exactly how full of shit they were. But that's exactly what Catherine was doing here.

I have never, in my life, been so hurt emotionally as I have by this one person who I loved and cherished above all others. Cat has been my lover, confidante, and best friend, and the person with whom I chose to create new life. I've worried about her, kept her safe to the best of my abilities, and supported her through every trial she's had to endure in all the time we've been together. But despite all my efforts, she's stuck a knife into me. That doesn't just disappoint, it burns, deep inside. And perhaps the hardest part of this is the fact that Cat doesn't seem to realise just how badly she's hurt me. She used to tell me how, when she was a teenager, she had an eating disorder. She was deeply unhappy. The one person who she thought she could turn to, who she needed for support, was her mother. But her mother seemed oblivious to it all, to the point of sewing dresses for Cat that would have fitted a prepubescent child. Cat used to despise her mother for failing to notice the bloody obvious, and yet here she is now, just as cold and heartless. Irony, eh?

I did everything possible to save our marriage. I even sacrificed my job prospects to support hers. Day in and day out, I looked after our boys, kept the house in order, and cooked meals, all to ensure that Catherine had a convenient life. So that she could go about keeping her career on track. Because that was the deal we'd made. Together. I supported her efforts to "find" herself, and sat by, trying to be OK about the fact that she was using another man to do so. I'm such a fucking idiot. And my reward? A kick in the teeth. I am absolutely disgusted by her behaviour.

Cat came downstairs after her bath and we talked. I somehow remained calm while she reiterated how shitty I am as a father. I could have said so many things in response, been so utterly hurtful and full of spite and venom. But what possible good would that do anyone? I had read and reread Cat's words. It was very clear that she wanted me gone. I'd served my purpose. I'd set her up in the life that she'd wanted for so long; her career was on track, she was about to be awarded a senior position and earn ridiculous amounts of money, she had a nice life in a quiet village, two happy and beautiful children, and she had a man who could address her every fantasy. But that man was not me. I was surplus to requirements. Yet again, redundant. So I kept quiet and I listened as she told me her plans, and her thoughts about the future. She would move out or I could move out. I told her I'd seen this coming for the past two years, and that I already had a rough idea of what I'd be doing. I said it made sense that I was the one who would move out, because I had no way of supporting the children financially. Catherine seemed relieved.

I told Cat that my plan involved moving back to Brazil. I said I wasn't yet sure whether it would be a permanent move (the issue of my involvement with the boys is still as pertinent as it was in my fictional entries, earlier in the diary), or just a temporary removal of myself from a toxic environment. As I sat there, hearing myself saying all of this, I realised that I will actually be doing what I have for so long been thinking about. I felt nauseous.

And just like that, the discussion was over.

In this one fateful evening, my entire world has imploded. It's now 3 a.m. and I'm not at all tired. Catherine is upstairs, fast asleep. Who knew that a love so strong could turn sour so incredibly quickly?

1 August 2011

Anger, hatred, disappointment, sadness … all useless emotions. Yet all so powerful, all conflicting inside me to find purchase at the top of my emotional ladder. I won't give in to any of them. To do so would mean that Catherine has won, that she has taken even more from me than I have already given. I need to be resilient, to realise that my old life is over, and to focus my attention on making myself strong enough to get through whatever is to come.

3 August 2011

I met Alice, earlier today. I didn't know why I needed to see her, or what I would say, but she deserved to know what's going on in my life. I owed her that, at least. She's been a shoulder to lean on, every step of the way, since we met.

I hadn't thought about what I would say to her, so I went in blind. And, as always, she shone for me. We sat on leather sofas in a bar. It was the middle of the afternoon, so there weren't too many other people around. I told Alice what had happened, and what my plans were. I think I had convinced myself that moving back to Brazil on a permanent basis was my only option. Yet the more we spoke, the more it became clear to me that Alice was not just a friend, not just a sub I'd had some fun with and who I could so readily cut ties with. We have a bond. We share so many things aside from kink; our sense of humour, our musical tastes, and a desire to write.

Alice has been self-employed for many years, but has long wished to travel the world, writing along the way. She playfully suggested the idea of putting me in her suitcase. We joked, but the more we talked, the more we realised what a strong possibility this actually was, based on our shared outlook on life and a mutual need to start afresh.

My head was spinning, but in a good way. Here was an option; a chance at heading down a completely new path, with an amazing woman. My only concern – as I mentioned to Alice – was that I was moving too fast; going from one relationship straight into another. It had occurred to both of us that I could be turning to Alice on the rebound, and that I hadn't had enough time to clear my head before moving on. We talked for hours. I never knew one pint of beer could last so long. Finally, when we'd been glared at by the waitress one too many times, we ordered coffee, and came to the conclusion that I had to stick to my plan, but with a new twist. I would go back to Brazil for at least three months and see my family, spend a bit of time in the sun, perhaps get to know São Paulo a bit, and then Alice would join me for a month or so. This would give me time to decide exactly what I want to do with my life, and to ascertain whether Alice and I are actually as compatible as we suspect. My plan has evolved, and now it includes a dynamic woman and exciting prospects. All of a sudden, for the first time in what feels like forever, my future doesn't seem so bleak after all.

7 August 2011

Catherine and I have decided to stay together for a month, while we get our shit sorted out. Cat has spoken to her niece, who is in a position to leave her temporary job in Paris to come to the United

Kingdom and au pair for a while. She is getting her affairs in order and should be arriving here in a few weeks. We'll move the house around before then, so that the children can get used to a few small changes. We both want there to be as little disruption to the boys' lives as possible. Aside from the fact that their father, who has looked after them every day for the past three years, will no longer be around. Not much of a change at all, then.

23 August 2011

I have seen Alice a few times in the past week or two, but have mainly spent my days sorting out financial matters, transferring various accounts into Cat's name, and packing up my stuff. I'm sure there will be a ton of legal stuff to think about, in time, but we'll have to address that as and when it happens. My main concern is that I'm absolutely fucking broke; I have no job, a negative bank balance, and not a single useful asset to my name. Who said life was dull, eh?

27 August 2011

Another letter to Cat, which I will probably end up not sending. Again. Why do I even bother writing this shit? The only purpose it serves is to frustrate me.

Pff. I'm including it here, anyway, if for no other reason than to have as a reference when the lawyers start beating on me to offer child maintenance.

Hey Cat.

You know what I feel like? I feel like a piece of toilet paper, which you've used and discarded in disgust once I'd served my purpose.

I encouraged you to return to your studies after you had quit because you didn't think it was the correct career choice. At the time you were in a high-paying job with a major corporation, and I convinced you to give that up and follow what had, for many years, been your dream. How fucking stupid was that *idea? Well done, me.*

I supported you throughout every step of your training, I gave you two wonderful, beautiful children, and I helped set you up in what will soon become your perfect life. And all I ever asked for was to be loved. I tried for so long to make you happy. I did everything I possibly could to facilitate that, and to keep us together. I was a good husband, and a good father.

As much as I wish you well in your future, I do that only because your success and happiness will directly affect the wellbeing of our boys. I hope, selfishly (for once), that you will someday look back on how you have treated me and come to see, clearly, what you have done to me and to the children. You have destroyed three lives in pursuit of your own happiness. Will you ever feel remorse, sorrow or regret for your actions? I can only hope so.

29 August 2011

We munched again, last night. I met Alice at the pub an hour before the official meeting time, and we had something to eat. Then followed yet another fantastic evening of chatting to old friends and getting to know new ones. What struck me was how much love there was in that room. I have found true friends here in this community that, just a few months ago, I never knew existed. These are people who care about me and have accepted me into their lives. I'm touched by their kindness and support. If my children are one reason for me returning to live in the UK, then Alice and the kink crowd are the other. I have no idea where Alice and I will live or how we'll support ourselves if I do return, but I believe we'll find a way.

Once again, irony slaps me upside the head. Three years ago, I knew nothing about the kink scene; what little I had seen or heard had been entirely negative, based on misinformation and bad press. Yet now I am a part of this world, and I feel more comfortable here than I have ever felt in the wider, vanilla society. I'm not a freak; I'm a decent, hard-working, intelligent human being. I treat others with kindness and respect. I love a good laugh, and I cry when I'm sad. I don't hate people because of the colour of the skin they happen to be born with, or for their sexual or religious orientations. I am not a monster. Unlike countless millions, who know nothing about kink, I no longer judge others based on false perceptions. And I am not violent. But I do enjoy having fun with other consenting adults, even if that fun involves ideas that are considered unconventional by many who have never experienced them. I am among friends; people who will not point fingers and judge me. I feel like I have come home. And it is a comfortable place.

2 September 2011

Our financial predicament was one of the reasons Catherine cited for us having to separate, and for all our woes. Yet, today, she met with someone at her bank, secured a large loan, consolidated all our debt, and paid off a bunch of outstanding bills. The fact that she will be earning a six-figure salary a few months from now means the loan will be paid back in very short order, and Cat's bank balance will soon be skyrocketing. So, it would seem that our disastrous financial situation is not so disastrous, after all. It would also seem – oh, and what a surprise this turned out to be – that it was almost an entirely insignificant factor for why Cat wanted the split. And finally (who would ever have guessed), all Cat has really wanted is to have another man's cock inside her. She was just bored with me, all along. Huge surprise.

3 September 2011: a letter, unsent

I have compiled all of my thoughts into a letter that I think explains a lot of what I'm feeling, right now. I have, over the past few years, written a few letters to Cat, yet not sent any of them for various reasons. Primarily, because I wanted to keep the peace, and not hurt this woman who I loved for so long. I came close to sending this latest letter, but – once again – I won't. Creating further animosity between us is pointless; I don't need the kids to see us treating each other with bitterness and resentment when we meet up in the future. So yet again I bitch, and moan, and cry into my diary, and hope that it will offer some level of comfort or relief. Sadly, it does neither.

Catherine,

You had your say in that fateful letter to me a few weeks ago. For all our talking, I never got to say a lot of things that have been on my mind for so long. Mainly because I never wanted to say them, especially since they were often tinged with anger. For the sake of our children, I have tried to keep my emotions buried, to be civil and calm and give the boys the impression that you are still close to my heart. Sadly, though, this is far from the case.

I don't think you have any idea of my true feelings, not now, and not over the past two years or more. These have been the hardest years of my life. I've never had to face anything like it before. Not only because you suddenly discovered your submissive side, but because, around the same time, I was made redundant. Us making the decision for me to stay home (the disruption to the kids' lives and your master's degree being the main factors in that disastrous agreement) meant that I effectively put my career on hold. Not that it was ever much of a "career", but it was all I had worked towards up until then. This was a joint decision, and something I do not and cannot regret. But having you throw that in my face as a reason for us separating was one of the most infuriating things I've ever had to hear. How fucking dare you?

Since we first met, I've encouraged you to return to your studies, to follow a vocation that would carry you through life. I have supported you every inch of the way. Not just emotionally, but financially – from way back when we first moved in together, until I lost my job. And then – yet again – I have that thrown back at me; the fact that our financial mess is somehow all my fault. That has made me incredibly resentful. I never planned to set you up in a career and sponge off you. I'd hoped you knew me better than that. Yet that's the impression I kept getting, for a long time. I'll take this opportunity to mention the fact that the master's degree only cost a mere three thousand pounds, not including books, travel, and accommodation. Perhaps I'll also point out that my brother lent you two thousand pounds to settle a tax deficit caused by your miscalculations – money that I will make damn sure I pay back to him someday.

Each time our finances were threatening to reach breaking point, I looked into part-time jobs – really shitty ones, like stacking shelves or waiting tables – in order to make a bit of cash and still be around for the kids. I also looked at various other job options, including working on oil rigs and joining the military. None of those were conducive to a home life that would benefit us or the boys in any way, aside from financially. And even then, the monetary reward would be minimal and could never compensate for the quality of life that the kids get from having a parent permanently looking after them. We discussed all of this, every time the subject of money arose. And we made a deal that I would stay home to look after the house and the boys, and you would be the breadwinner. Just like millions of other families. Every decision I made was done to facilitate an easier life for the children. Ironically, it turns out that exactly the opposite is happening.

As to my handling of James, yes, I have been harsh with him. I have done my damnedest to raise him no differently to how I did Robert, who has turned out to be the happiest, most wonderfully kind-hearted little person I could ever have hoped for. I know James will follow suit. He's naughty. I get that. I was the same when I was his age, apparently. But dealing with that each and every day (and most nights) takes a heavy toll. As you have probably noticed, I've eased off, considerably, since we had our talk. As I said to you, all it took was you saying something. It wasn't that hard. But I feel that, yet again, this was some way in which you could shift the blame onto me for our marriage falling apart.

That evening in the restaurant, while we were on holiday, when you told me about Simon, was one of the most traumatic events

I've had to face. I knew then that our marriage was in deep trouble. Yet, since that night, I have done everything in my power, and pursued every possible route, to give you what you need. I have served as a maid, an au pair, and a friend, through all of this. And the only thing I ever wanted was to fix us. I have fought tirelessly to make us work, to let you have the life you want, but also to keep us together – not just for the sake of the kids, but because I loved you, more deeply than I can say. I was even willing to let another man put his hands all over you, long before I met someone who could offer me the same level of companionship.

Your constant reassurances that you weren't at all like my ex were an absolute farce. We both knew that, the very moment you met Simon in person, it would be over between us. And yet you still went ahead. Both you and Tracey had proclaimed, over and over, that you never wanted anyone else. You both wanted to grow old with me. Neither of you would ever, in a hundred years, even contemplate being attracted to a muscled man, far preferring someone tall and lean like me. Uh huh. Sure. Yet, oh look, both of you ended up chasing after meatheads who spend all of their spare time in a gym. I have never once abused you, verbally, mentally, or physically. I have always been faithful, and your closest friend and confidant. Receiving a slap in the face for all my effort tells me a lot about what you really think of me.

For all that you used to explain how

oblivious your mother was to your mental decline, all those years ago, you have done the same thing to me for so long. But if blaming me alleviates your guilt somewhat, then so be it. I always said I'd take the fall if it meant keeping your nose clean, and I still mean that. It was your decision to tell our friends and family that you'd met someone first (albeit sans details). That, at least, is something.

I realise that our marriage has been failing for a long time. I now accept that. But for you to cast the blame on me is unforgivable. I have done everything I possibly could to keep us together, and have offered you the life you want with no expectations in return. I refuse to keep this resentment bottled up for the rest of my days. I want us to remain civil for the sake of the boys, but I can't pretend I'm not disappointed and angry. What you have done to me, and our little family, cuts deep, and can never be forgotten.

I do wish you the best on your career path, if only for Rob and Jamie's sake. It helps me to know that I have played a huge part in facilitating their future financial stability. What I would like is a reassurance that they will be spending more time with you than they have in the past few years. In turn I will do my utmost to see them as much as possible. In fact, I am already putting plans in place to enable this to happen. I will continue to act civilly toward you, for the boys' sake.

I haven't said any of this over the past few

weeks because I've wanted the anger to go away. I've focussed on the positives, and tried to banish any negative thoughts and emotions because they're unhelpful. But I find I've been bottling them up, and I refuse to do that any longer. I'm tired of always looking after other people, of being aware of their feelings and not tending to my own. There is no longer any danger of me losing you due to a careless remark, hence why I'm telling you all of this.

I want us to be able to get along, to appear happy when we see each other in front of the children. And, in time, I hope we can settle into an easy friendship, once all of this has passed. But you have hurt me, incredibly badly, and that is going to take a very long time to heal.

I would like to be able to wish you best of luck and happiness with Simon, but that would be disingenuous; for all his support and best intentions, he will forever be the man who took my wife away from me. But I do truly wish you luck in your future. I know you'll have a successful life, and I'm sorry I couldn't be a part of that. I feel robbed of years of my time and effort in the support I've given. But, at least, the kids will benefit from it, and that's a comforting thought.

David

5 September 2011

As these final few days in my house and with my children come to a close, so does my diary. I have a return plane ticket to Brazil, departing in less than a week. I'll be staying with my brother and sister-in-law near Rio for the first month, and then I'll be travelling down to São Paulo, to spend the next two months bunking down in my cousin's spare room. Alice will join me for the final month. The plan is for me to relax, and perhaps explore São Paulo a bit, to get a feel for it. Then, when Alice arrives, we will both explore it further. We'll have an extremely budgeted holiday, and then return to Britain so that I can be back with my boys. Or, at least, near them. Before we return, Alice and I will need to work out exactly what we'll be doing with our lives. She could continue with her job as a consultant, and I have the option to start looking for jobs in IT again. We're both extremely keen on writing fiction, so maybe we'll start doing that, and live off the charity of Alice's parents, until such time as we find fame and fortune. Alternatively, we may both simply fall in love with São Paulo, and decide to settle there. The downside of that plan would be that I'd get to see the kids a lot less frequently, probably once a year on average, if they were able to fly out during their summer holidays. I have no idea if I could last that long without seeing my babies, so that would be the selfish choice, and one I'm less inclined to want to pursue. But the option is there.

Whatever I – we – decide, my world is about to change, radically. I hope I'm strong enough to handle whatever challenges await me. I hope that Alice and I can forge a successful life together. Most of all, I hope that my children will continue to be the happy, well-mannered little people that Cat and I have raised them to be. I want them to be OK, more than anything else. I have to trust that Catherine will do her best in that regard.

What does my future hold in store? Good things, I hope. It's all anyone can wish for. What lies ahead is a blank slate. I have never sought wealth or fame; all I ever wanted was to be happy, and to make others happy. I'm hoping that my new friends, and my new life in a kinky environment, will allow all of that to happen.

As for Cat … In truth, as I've already reiterated far too many times, right now, I despise the woman. She has destroyed a life that I worked very hard to build, and she has shown very little remorse. Worse, she has cast the blame for the failure of our marriage onto me, even after all the shit I went through to try to make it work. I can never forgive what she's done. But any feelings of anger or bitterness that I have toward her will need to be cast aside. I need to create a new life with what remains of my willpower. Alice is my woman now, and kink is my world. As terrifying as that all is, it's also incredibly exciting. A new life awaits me, and I am nervous yet strangely eager to find out where it will lead.

Part Eight
Epilogue and Other Bits

Epilogue

I do, of course, appreciate that there are two sides to any story. What I have chronicled here is obviously just one side: mine. Whatever Catherine's faults, she has had no chance to defend her thoughts or actions. I'm sure that, if she did, her words would put many of mine into some sort of context whereby much of my ranting would seem unreasonable, or even irrational. But I can't write that for her. What I have written is presented as facts from my perspective; it is my interpretation of events as they took place. Although the vast majority of people reading this will in all likelihood never meet her, please try not to judge Cat as harshly as I have. If I realise one thing after all my years of observing this species, it is that nobody has any right to point fingers.

To anyone out there who finds themselves in a similar situation to that which I have faced with Catherine, I wish you luck getting through it. Perhaps your bond will be stronger than what I believed mine to be with Cat. Your circumstances could be different, and perhaps you'll find a way to fix what you have together. I really hope that is the case. I did all that I possibly could in order to save my marriage. But although I prolonged the inevitable, in the end, it just didn't work. Maybe your partner will decide that your future together is more important than their own happiness; perhaps if you have children, your partner may decide that having a secure family environment is more important than satisfying their own lust. I'm not a natural, so I don't entirely know what that lust feels like; I can't judge, because I have no way of knowing what it is I'm judging. And I have no right to judge, anyway. None of us do. All I can say is that we can all only do what we feel is right, and try hard not to hurt others along the way. If any of what I have written is of any help to anyone, even to simply let you know that you're not alone in having to face this utterly mindblowing revelation from a loved one, then I've done something useful. Good luck to you getting through it unscathed.

On Misconceptions

As I have mentioned a few times in my writing, it is a sad fact that BDSM is, by and large, considered abhorrent due to misinformation. This is something that continues to enrage me.

At the time of writing this, I am staying with my brother for a few weeks. Out of sheer boredom (yes, I know I should be trying to further my writing ambitions by actually – oh, I don't know, maybe *writing* something), I have been perusing my brother's bookshelves. His taste is somewhat more mainstream than mine, and he enjoys crime thrillers. Over the past three weeks, I have randomly chosen three different books by three different authors. I managed to wade through the first two, but the third one, regrettably, has proven too much. There are only so many sad clichés that one can endure, only so many homicides that one can pretend to be intrigued by, only so many romantic-but-not-until-the-very-end, beautiful-yet-slightly-flawed cop/lawyer partnerships that one can stomach, and only so many "unexpected" twists one can be astounded by.

What pissed me off, though, was that in each and every one of these novels, SM played a part. And in each case, it was used as an instrument of evil, associated with torture, and used alongside such words as "depraved" and "twisted". How absolutely, disappointingly fucking typical. And how completely indicative of how the BDSM community is perceived. Yet again, ignorance rears its ugly head. Books like those I read are a dime a dozen, yet they serve only to further perpetuate a lie; that the practice of BDSM is somehow seedy, degenerate, and violent. Uninformed and indiscriminate use of SM as a villainous element does kink a great disservice.

I honestly hope that some of what I described in my writing – once I had actually taken the time and made an effort to learn what D/s was truly all about – will help to dispel some of the more irritating and predictable misconceptions created by crime writers looking for an easy target.

I had a conversation, a short while back, with a vanilla friend of mine. I told him what I was up to, and what my new life involved. I choose my friends carefully, so I wasn't terribly surprised that he was, on the whole, unfazed. What did concern him, though, was the issue of safety. How, he wondered, was any submissive ever really "safe" when playing in private? He got the Dominant/submissive thing; he understood when I explained to him how a connection is established between two people who, in time and with trust, become play partners. But I had a lot more trouble explaining how, when two people first start playing together, a submissive is essentially "safe" having been tied up and gagged. Humans are curious things, and we've all heard stories of someone's personality changing in seconds, to the point of them acting like a stranger. On a "normal" date, this is a frightening concept. But add to the mixture some shackles and a bunch of sharp implements, and things could get a whole lot messier. My friend asked me whether this sort of thing ever happens in kink. I could only reply that it probably did. But, in my opinion (and based on my limited knowledge), it probably happened a hell of a lot less than in the vanilla world. Why? Because, for the most part, kink and the practice of BDSM is a communal business. We police ourselves. And we adhere to a strict code. Even the most hardened anarchists among us are aware of the first rule of D/s: "SSC", which stands for "Safe, Sane, and Consensual". It has also come to be known as "RACK", which is "Risk Aware Consensual Kink". Consent is primary. Practitioners of BDSM do not abuse children. They do not abuse animals. They do not do anything to anyone who does not wish something done to them. It is frowned upon to consume alcohol or drugs of any sort prior to a play session although, of course, everyone is entitled to do what they please within the confines of their own home and with willing partners. If there are incidents of abuse, or anything that smells even remotely non-consensual, then the perpetrators are given one hell of a virtual beating, and not in a good way. My friend was sceptical as to the effectiveness of this method of self-regulation within the community. And, I must admit, so am I. But beneath it all, we're just people. Normal people, I hasten to add; people with jobs and kids and mortgages and shit, just like anyone else. But when we get horny, we like something a little different from the standard, 'Brace yerself, Sheila.' And, so what? Is what we do affecting anyone else in any way? I don't think so.

We use common sense and instinct in every aspect of our lives. There are, no doubt, rogue elements within the kink community, just as in every other walk of life. However, I would dare to venture that these are, in all probability, far fewer and further between here than in the vanilla world.

One hears of teenagers getting blind drunk and landing themselves in all sorts of trouble every weekend on the streets of Britain. Newspaper headlines are littered with stories of spousal and child abuse. Political, religious, and celebrity figures are continually receiving slaps on the wrist for having used their status to get away with all sorts of indecent behaviour. Whereas thus far, in my (admittedly brief) time within the kink community, I have heard of only one incident of non-consensual and inappropriate touching, and that involved alcohol. The abusers involved were very quickly named and shamed, and are no longer welcome within the scene.

I can only hope that something of what I have tried to convey in this book with regard to the nature of kink will play a part in helping the uninformed to perhaps understand, if not accept, just a little bit more of what BDSM is really all about.

Acknowledgements

The disclosure to some of our closest friends (after some very careful and tentative thought and great consideration) that Catherine and I were involved in D/s relationships broke some of those friendships, yet strengthened others. The fact that we were able to conduct what may be regarded as "illicit affairs" outside our relationship resulted in us being shunned by people who we once considered enlightened, which was incredibly difficult for both of us to accept. But to those who stood by and supported us, I thank you unreservedly.

To all of my kinky friends, many of whom took me into their lives and their homes and talked about anything and everything over numerous cups of tea – you know who you are – I thank you wholeheartedly. This journey of discovery could have turned out so very differently but for your input and support. I have met some amazingly wonderful people over the past few months; people who, just a few years ago, I would have regarded as freaks and weirdoes, thanks to my limited understanding of the lifestyle.

Deepest thanks to the (for the most part) caring, polite, and intelligent online BDSM community whose help was crucial in guiding a frightened, uninformed, and very vanilla newcomer. Thanks in particular to the websites Xeromag and Fetlife for making my journey easier.

A word or two regarding "Catherine". Looking back on what I've written, I have expressed various – often extreme – emotions. Yet, through it all, I never wanted to hate the woman. She was a friend and a lover for many years. What she discovered inside her was something that has always existed. She chose to embrace it, where perhaps others may have fought it, thereby denying themselves the opportunity to explore what made them tick. For this I admire her, but at the same time I curse her, because it destroyed what we had; it blew apart our family structure and left our children with a broken home, and a future without a regularly present father. I can never forgive that. I don't ever want my children to know what Catherine has done to me and to us as a family. That won't help anyone. And so, I have to focus on the future, to live my life and try to find happiness again. I will never again trust the woman who was my wife. I will never again feel tenderness and love for her, as I did for so many years. What I will feel is the disappointment of betrayal, and a deep sadness that what could have been a wonderful, happy life with our two beautiful children has been demolished by her actions and decisions. Having come to understand, ever so slightly more, about what she is going through, I guess I should be happy for her. I'm pleased that Catherine has been able to scratch an itch that has for so long bothered her. I'm just miserable about the fact that it had to happen at all.

And my most profound thanks, of course, to "Simon", for taking time out of his busy schedule to smack my wife's arse.

A final word of thanks and love: to my sexy, gorgeous submissive, Alice, for being a pillar in the turmoil of a marriage in ruin. Thank you for encouraging me, right up to the end, to try to make things work out with Cat; a lesser person may not have understood what I was going through. Thank you for helping me discover the hidden Dom inside me, and for offering me everything I could ever have dreamed of in a play partner.

As of this writing, I have returned to my native Brazil on a three-month hiatus. I am tidying up the last bits of writing on this diary as I wait for Alice to join me. Once she does so, we will be travelling together, seeing a few parts of this beautiful country, and then embarking on a life together that will hopefully involve travel to various other picturesque parts of the planet – with regular stops to the United Kingdom in order to visit two little people who I love more dearly than anything else in this world. Alice has helped to show me that life doesn't have to stop due to unforeseen trauma; that there is always light, no matter how dark the path may seem. Our D/s relationship is stronger than it has ever been, and now our "real" relationship is about to begin. Can we incorporate the two? Only time will tell. But I have faith in a future of my own making. And with a woman who I know wants to please me, to love me, and to treat me in a way I deserve. I can only offer her the same in return.

Afterword

BDSM is a many varied thing. There are practices within this lifestyle which confuse and repel even the most hardened among us; again, things that *other* people do. However, most of us respect the right of everyone to do as they please, so long as nobody outside of their scene is being affected. And, obviously, so long as anyone *within* their scene is safe and has consented to be a part of it. While I may not be into some of the more extreme elements, it is not my place to judge others; "your kink is not my kink", as the saying goes. A few people within my circle of friends are into some of the more hardcore kink. Yet they are one and all the loveliest, kindest, most friendly people I could ever wish to know. What they do in private does not affect me. It does not rub off on me. Most of them won't even discuss it with me, only making vague reference to their activities, when I curiously push for more information.

Kink is not about pain; it is about pleasure. While this is sometimes achieved via methods which include inflicting pain, it is nigh on impossible to explain to anyone who is not themselves submissive how such a thing can be pleasurable. Submissives feel pain in the same way that the rest of us do. They do not enjoy pain for its own sake. Yet within the context of submitting to someone, of entrusting their bodies and minds to another person, they can achieve a euphoric state that is as close to bliss as is humanly possible. I doubt that I will ever achieve this level of ecstasy, but I am satisfied in the knowledge that I can do this for others.

For all that though, I'm dangerous. I recognise this fact. As someone who has been "vanilla" my whole life, and who has only (relatively) recently been introduced to a new phenomenon which I've barely begun to explore, I'm probably the last person who should be writing anything on the subject of D/s because I don't have any understanding about the psychological aspect of it. And that aspect is huge.

I've played, and it's been fun and arousing. But I don't honestly believe that I have come close to understanding the emotional impact it's having on the women I've interacted with (or, in fact, what impact it should be having, while I'm admonishing them for their perceived transgressions). Real Dominance and submission goes beyond simple porn, so much deeper than a quick thrill. It is a place where physical sexual gratification is often the very least important factor in an encounter. As someone who is not intrinsically vested in this dynamic, it would be hypocritical for me to think I could bestow my "knowledge" on others. As such, everything I've written in this diary has been – obviously – a chronicle; my own real-life tale of a love that made me attempt to overcome huge odds, and how I survived the experience.

Sadly, I cannot imagine the emotional distress that so many people – latent Dominants or submissives – must have suffered over the centuries; people who have not had anyone to share their pain and turmoil with. Some may have been fortunate enough to identify the source of their anguish, to confront it, and, perhaps with the help of peers, embrace this brave new world. But there must be so many thousands of others who, throughout history, have gone to their graves miserable and none the wiser as to what's been happening in their minds. I truly mourn for those people, and am saddened by their unfulfilled lives. Hopefully what I have written here will help a few people to understand that what they're experiencing is not unique and does not in any way make them inferior to others (and thanks to the millions of so-called normal people for perpetuating that stereotype). BDSM is not kiddie porn. And while, for some practitioners, it may involve simulated rape scenes or what most people would consider violent acts, if what is done is consensual and safe, then for God's sake, let people just live their fucking lives in peace. I really don't think that's too much to ask.

This has been one hell of a journey. Thank you for taking it with me.

Xcite

For more information about David Wade and other Xcite books, please visit

www.xcitebooks.co.uk